EMMA STIRLING

◆

A SUMMER
ENGAGEMENT

Complete and Unabridged

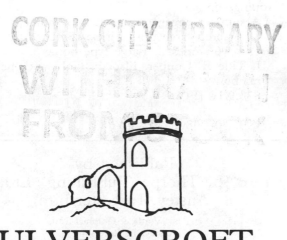

ULVERSCROFT
Leicester

First published in Great Britain in 1996 by
Severn House Publishers Limited, Surrey

Originally published in 1981 under the title
'The Gold and the Rainbow' by
Elspeth Couper

First Large Print Edition
published 1997
by arrangement with
Severn House Publishers Limited, Surrey

British Library CIP Data

Stirling, Emma
    A summer engagement.—Large print ed.—
Ulverscroft large print series: romance
1. Love stories 2. Large type books
I. Title II. Couper, Elspeth. Gold and the
rainbow
823.9'14 [F]

ISBN 0–7089–3765–9

Published by
2411 F. A. Thorpe (Publishing) Ltd.
Anstey, Leicestershire

Set by Words & Graphics Ltd.
Anstey, Leicestershire
Printed and bound in Great Britain by
T. J. International Ltd., Padstow, Cornwall

This book is printed on acid-free paper

1

KERRI watched as the green bus gathered speed, crossed the old stone bridge and vanished along the road leading to the village. It was spring, the best time of the year in High Linton.

The grass in the wide fields that stretched on each side of her was verdant, luxuriant and sweet-smelling after the night's rain. She loved this place. She knew every inch of the countryside; where to find the wild violets that peeped shyly through almost before winter was over, the swift-flowing streams where she could walk quietly, meeting no one, stopping to gaze at her reflection in the mossy-brown stream, fascinated by the darting dragonflies that skimmed the water.

She had wandered these pathways as a child, then clinging to the hand of her brother, three years older than herself; sometimes, as she grew older, with a boyfriend. But she preferred to be alone. Solitude didn't worry her. Here especially.

It was a place of beauty, withstanding all attempts to obliterate it in favour of a new bridge and road. The only concession to modern-day living was the bus she could still hear in the distance, gears protesting as it climbed the steep hill to the village.

For the past three years she had caught that bus each morning on her way to work in the travel agency in the town.

But she wasn't going to work today.

Today, she felt, was the beginning of a new life. She should have done it long ago, instead of going on, day after dreary day, in the same old round.

She felt restless, vague longings making her suddenly and inexplicably dissatisfied with her life. She didn't really know what had happened. She had always thought she was content with her job in the travel agency and would stay there for as long as she needed to. She was passably good at her work, helpful, and competent, and the customers liked her. Then, just over a week ago, for no reason that she could think of, she suddenly decided that she hated the thought of spending the next untold number of years in this place with its desks, telephones and large colourful posters depicting scenes from exotic places that were, to her, only names.

The feeling that she had had enough came after an elderly couple who had been downright rude, who had waved all her helpful suggestions aside, had finally asked to see the manager, giving the impression that she had gone out of her way to be unco-operative.

Later, as they walked out of the office, she had gone into the manager's office and, before he had time to speak, had given her notice. Later, back at her own desk, she had quivered at the monumental and, she thought later, rather hasty step she had taken.

All that week she had dithered. Should she stay on, or should she leave things as they were? But on the last day she had walked out of the place without a backward glance.

Now she was free, free as a bird, to do and go where she liked. Even if, she thought wryly, the idea of being without a job did give her a feeling of guilt. She had told her mother she would take a few weeks off before looking for another position. She owed herself a bit of time, spent doing exactly as she liked after three years pandering to other people's wants.

She couldn't expect her mother to keep her for nothing. But there were plenty of jobs. Weren't the evening papers filled with them? Jobs for shop assistants, office workers, waitresses in the local cafés. But nothing, she had to admit, that excited her. Wouldn't it be nice, just for once, to consider something different?

Before supper she would walk across the common to the stationer's in the High Street, buy a newspaper, seriously consider what was on offer and tomorrow set her mind on doing something about it. Finding a seat to herself on the peaceful common, she opened the paper and scanned the Situations Vacant columns. The first flickerings of hope had faded long before she reached the end of the columns. There were any amount of jobs to be had, that was true, but nothing that really appealed to her. Surely, if she

4

held out for another week she would see *some*thing she wanted amongst all those ads for domestic servants, secretaries, shop assistants, dental assistants, and what have you?

Even the out-of-the-ordinary jobs, like someone to live in a cottage in the country and look after the owner's cat and budgie while they were away, or someone to fetch and carry for an elderly lady for two weeks while her son was on the Continent on business, didn't tempt her.

Dejectedly, Kerri began to fold the paper when a few lines caught her eye. Tucked away toward the end of the columns, in a private box of its own, she read 'Responsible woman to look after a young schoolgirl on the island of Lessane in the Pacific Islands for the duration of summer vacation. Ring Westleigh 371.'

The excitement that she had thought dead stirred in her once more. Her heart began to jump. She felt a headiness, such as when she had partaken of too much champagne at a friend's wedding. Wasn't this just the chance she was waiting for? Something different? Oh, certainly something different! Would she appear responsible enough to whoever was interviewing her to be in charge of a schoolgirl — the advertisement hadn't mentioned the child's age — for the whole of the summer! It was worth trying, anyway. And it would depend on how long the advert had been in the paper. The position might already have gone. It sounded too enticing not to have had dozens of applicants after it.

Well, anyway, a phone call wouldn't hurt, and the advertiser could always say, sorry, but the position is already filled, couldn't they?

Spurred by the vision of golden beaches, palm trees and wide blue lagoons, she hurried back to the house, closing the door of the small room her father used as a study, and, lifting the receiver, dialled the number purposefully.

There was a click and a woman's voice came on the line. For a moment Kerri wanted to hang up, then telling herself not to be an idiot, she said breathlessly, "I'm phoning about the advertisement. The one about . . . "

The woman's voice cut in abruptly,

silencing her. "Will you please hold on. I will ask Mr Prentice to come to the phone."

Kerri, her nerves taut, waited, telling herself there was still time to hang up, then telling herself not to be a coward. At least she could *listen* to the man, couldn't she? In all probability the job would be gone, anyway . . .

Then, just as the last remnants of her courage was deserting her, a voice, deep and very solemn, said in her ear, "Good evening! Dominic Prentice speaking."

Knowing that she either had the chance of making a complete fool of herself by backing out, or going ahead with the venture she had started, she said, very coolly, "Good evening, Mr Prentice. I'm calling about the situation you have advertised in this evening's paper. My name is Kerri Matheson."

"Ah, yes!" Was there a hint of irascibility in his tone, a thread of ill-humour? She had no time to decide before the voice went on, "Good evening, Miss Matheson. I presume it *is* Miss? I require someone without commitments, you understand. Certainly someone who is married need not apply."

Why, she thought, hadn't he stated that in his advert? She said, crisply, "No, Mr Prentice, I'm not married."

"Good. Now," and the impatience she had first noticed in his voice sharpened. "I have very little time to waste on this matter. My brother, who is an archaeologist, has had to go out to Lebanon. There have been some important excavations discovered there recently and his presence is required for the summer. His daughter Jane, my niece, is at school in Kent and as her school closes for the summer vacation in a few days' time something must be done about her. Now, the problem is this. I have arranged to spend some time on the island of Lessane. I am a writer and I'm doing a book on the island's history. As I will be kept fairly busy most of the day I have decided a companion for Jane would be the answer. Although the person I choose must be young, she must also be responsible, for she will be in sole charge of my niece. Do I make myself clear, Miss Matheson?"

Kerri nodded, realised he couldn't

see her and said, "Yes, Mr Prentice, I understand perfectly."

"And you would be prepared to undertake such a task? You would be capable of controlling a fairly spoiled sixteen-year-old?"

Sixteen! she thought, wryly. Hardly the child he makes her out to be.

She said, "I'm sure I would, Mr Prentice."

She heard his grunt, then there was a moment's silence as though he wrote something down. After this he wasted no time in getting down to business. He asked her a few brief questions about her schooling and her parents. Seeming satisfied at her answers, he went on, "Of course, I shall have to see you personally."

She bridled a little at the imperiousness of his tone, but her own voice was calm as she replied, "I understand. I could come whenever it is convenient."

"No time is convenient, but I suppose the sooner I get this thing sorted out the sooner I'll be relieved of it." He made it sound as though the whole thing was distasteful to him and Kerri felt brief pity for the young girl who was his niece. His voice *sounded* young, but that didn't mean a thing.

He was in all probability some unsociable, middle-aged bachelor who lived alone and had an aversion to youth and anything that threatened to disturb his seclusion.

In a way she understood how he felt. Hadn't she felt the same on those walks by the river, dreading the thought that someone might intrude on the wonderful peacefulness and upset things?

Still, there was no need for him to be so abrupt, so — so brusque about everything. It wasn't his niece's fault that her father had been summoned away, leaving her uncle to determine what to do with her for the summer. And if her father was anything like his brother, then she doubly pitied the girl with two such men in charge of her upbringing.

Briefly she wondered what had happened to the girl's mother, then pushed the thought away as the voice in her ear said, "Do you know Westleigh at all? We live in the red brick house on the corner of the square. You can't possibly miss it. Take a taxi. I'll reimburse you for the fare."

"All right," she said. "Do you want me to come now?"

It would be dark in another hour. She realised this as she turned her head to glance out of the window.

He must have realised this, too, for he said, "No, that won't be necessary. Tomorrow will do. Make it fairly early and then if you are suitable we can get everything — passport, vaccinations and suchlike — sorted out without wasting too much time." Then, as an afterthought, "What *about* a passport? I presume you have one, Miss Matheson. And that your vaccinations and so forth are up to date."

Having worked in the travel agency and being able to make short trips to the Continent at a discount, she could answer both questions truthfully.

"Yes, I'm fine where that sort of thing is concerned."

"Good. Then I'll expect you tomorrow morning. Goodnight."

His leave-taking was so abrupt that she was left with the receiver still in her hand, staring at it in disbelief. She dropped it back on its rest as her mother's

11

voice sounded from the passage outside. "Kerri? Are you in there, love? Supper's ready."

"Coming, Mum." Excitement exploded inside her. She had the job. She was sure of that, even though she hadn't actually seen the man yet. She couldn't honestly say she cared much for the sound of him, but if he was to be busy all day he wouldn't really bother her, and she was sure she and the girl, Jane, would get on famously.

She would need new clothes, summer things that were light and gay, that would go with the life of a Pacific island. It all sounded so unreal she thought she must be dreaming until, over supper, she began to tell her family and then the real excitement came.

Her mother put one hand over her mouth, gazing at her wide-eyed above it. "Oh, Kerri, do you think you should? You don't know what you might be letting yourself in for . . . "

Her brother laughed. "She means white slavers and all that jazz, kid. I don't think you need worry about that, Ma. Our Kerri's not exactly the stuff of which seductresses are made. Too skinny for one thing."

He grinned at her over the table, ignoring their mother's gasp of indignation. "Besides," he went on, "Dominic Prentice is a quite well-known name in the literary world. He writes, I believe, on archaeological findings, and his brother is equally well known. I'm sure with his reputation, Ma, you need have no fear about Kerri's honour."

The following morning Kerri was up early, throwing off her shortie nightie and glancing at her collection of dresses, skirts and slacks with a frown. Filled with indecision, she pulled first one garment from its hanger, then another until her mother, coming in the room behind her, said, "Why not this one, love?" taking out a pale blue cotton dress with a tiny white spotted pattern and crisp white Peter Pan collar. "It's fresh and young and I've always liked it on you."

Kerri's frown deepened. That was the trouble! She didn't particularly *want* to look young. Not *too* young, anyway. Mr Prentice had hinted that, although youth might not be a disadvantage, he was looking for someone both steady and trustworthy. She didn't want to turn up looking like *ingénue* from some 1930s play, and, in her opinion, the dress her mother had suggested made her feel, if not look, just that.

Her mother had made it for her at the beginning of the summer and, not wanting to hurt her feelings, Kerri had worn it a couple of times. Now, quite honestly, she didn't think it was quite what she wanted for the interview with her future employer.

She said, hesitantly, "Well, I don't know, Mum. I thought a skirt and blouse and this jacket . . . " pulling forward a tweed skirt and green silk blouse with a tie collar and the tan suede jacket that went so well with them.

Without a word her mother thrust the dress back into the wardrobe but Kerri could see by her face that she was smarting. "You see, Mum," she went on hurriedly, slipping one arm about her mother's ample waist and giving her a quick hug, "Mr Prentice said he wanted a responsible person to look after his niece, and that dress does make me look very young. If I get the job I'll certainly take it with me. It would be ideal to wear in hot weather."

Appeased, her mother smiled, returning the hug. "Of course, dear. I understand. And there won't be any doubts about you getting it, I'm sure. I think, apart from being so far away from home, it will be just what you're looking for."

Her brother telephoned for a taxi and within minutes it was there, parked outside their front gate. Giving herself a last hasty glance in the mirror, she felt that the tweed skirt, the neat green blouse and suede jacket, into the collar of which she had tucked a bright lemon silk scarf, leaving the ends to float free, gave her style and dignity. The neat brown walking-shoes she had chosen, together with the more severe style in which she had arranged her chestnut auburn hair, taking it into a smooth chignon at the nape of her neck, made her feel elegant.

As the taxi moved away, taking the main road to Westleigh, her mind full of the conversation that had taken place on the telephone between herself and Dominic Prentice, the fields on either side, scattered with wild flowers, even a glimpse of the sea, far away to the west, were lost on her as she thought about the coming interview.

She couldn't really believe her good fortune. A summer spent on the island of Lessane, with its fabulous beaches and blue lagoon! It seemed too good to be true. Something that happened to other people but never to oneself. She reminded herself that she hadn't *got* the job yet, so it was no good counting her chickens, as her mother was fond of saying. But she had a feeling, an intuition, that she would. Still, she wanted to pinch herself to make sure she wasn't dreaming. Ideas began to tumble around in her head.

What would the girl, Jane, be like? What, indeed, would Dominic Prentice himself be like? She had had the impression of cool arrogance, of an inability to suffer fools gladly. Steeped in his writings of ancient cities and lost cultures, would he be interested only in palming off his niece to some suitable person and concentrating on his creative activities?

The taxi was approaching the outskirts of Westleigh, slowing now to go through the town. At last they stopped outside tall iron gates that stood guard at a long driveway that in turn led up to a massive front door.

The driver climbed out, swung open the gates and then drove slowly through, stopping at the steps that led up to the front door. He leaned over his shoulder to say, "'Ere you are, miss. Want me to wait for you?"

Kerri hesitated. She had to get back, didn't she? The driver might as well wait, although, as she explained, she didn't know how long she would be. He smiled, a middle-aged man with daughters of his own. "That's orl right, miss. I don't mind waiting. Be a change from driving."

Kerri thanked him and got out. The door stood closed and inhospitable-looking, solid oak that looked as though it had been there for a hundred years and probably had. She lifted her hand and pulled the iron ring which was on one side. The deep booming tones of the

17

bell echoed inside the house, followed a few minutes later by slow footsteps and then a woman stood in the doorway, peering out.

She looked as though she might have been there as long as the oak door, her figure bent, her hands gnarled, full of arthritis.

"Good morning," Kerri said, a little nervously. "I'm Miss Matheson. Mr Prentice asked me to call and see him about the job in the paper."

The woman scowled, as though she didn't approve of anything her master did, but gestured her in, then led her across a gorgeous Persian carpet of reds and blues that almost covered the wide hall. She pushed open the door of a room opposite.

"Wait there," she said, her tone stiff and unfriendly, her eyes full of censure as she took in Kerri's pale pink lipstick and the faint trace of eye-shadow. She had worn the minimum of make-up, for with her pale creamy skin, the penalty of her hair colour, she looked too pale without it.

Her face was a perfect oval, the brows

finely marked, blue eyes that could darken to the deepest, most sensual violet. An incredibly thick fringe of dark lashes, and seeing her for the first time, most people were immediately struck by those bewitching eyes.

She fidgeted now in the silence as the woman closed the door, leaving her alone. The room into which she had been shown was large and gloomy, the furniture massive, of a much earlier age. It looked sad and neglected, and Kerri could imagine the room in Victorian times teeming with children, a huge log fire in the grate. Servants in neat black and white uniforms flitting like shadows to do their mistress's bidding.

She allowed herself to drift into a dream of old-fashioned Christmasses, the kind that Dickens had described, with a tree drooping under the presents for the crowd of children, music and laughter and the lady of the house sitting by the fire in her wide crinoline, administering to her family and guests . . .

"Miss Matheson!"

The voice was curt, impatient, and she started, colour flooding her cheeks. She looked up to see a tall man standing in the open doorway. His gaze was fixed intently upon her. The piercing quality of that gaze made her flush deepen. Suddenly the room seemed very warm, stuffy almost, and she felt herself invaded by a strange emotion, half excitement, half dread that she didn't think she liked.

She didn't think she liked, too, this tall imposing stranger who gazed at her so disdainfully. Before she could speak, she heard him sigh, then say, his impatience very evident now, "*Are* you the person I spoke to on the telephone last evening?"

"Yes. My name is Kerri Matheson." Kerri managed to get the words out in a steady voice, although she felt fierce resentment stirring at his brusque manner. "I — I followed your advice and took a taxi. I asked the driver to wait. I hope you don't mind . . . ?"

"Not at all. Those were my instructions, were they not? But now that you *are* here, do you suppose we could get on with the task in hand? I am an extremely busy man and have very little time to stand and gossip."

Kerri stood very still, glaring at him. Dark grey eyes fringed with black lashes gazed into hers. His hair was dark, his features too hard to be called handsome, although she supposed when he smiled they would soften and lose some of their craggy look.

If he ever smiled! Looking at him now she couldn't see much chance of that. Going over to a wing-backed chair upholstered in crimson velvet he stood waiting, gesturing her to the one opposite. "Do sit down, Miss Matheson. We have very little time to complete our arrangements for the summer and I still have to pick my niece up at school. Now, perhaps, you would be good enough to tell me a little more about yourself. Where you have been working and other relevant things."

Her lips twisted dryly. She wouldn't call working for the past three years in the office of a travel agency 'relevant', but she supposed she had better confess. He listened to her hesitant version of her years since leaving school, frowning, tapping impatiently on one knee with strong brown fingers.

"And you think, with this kind of background, you could keep track of a girl of sixteen for the summer in a place like Lessane?"

She looked at him, taking in the strong rugged features, the eyes that were as cold as the winter skies above the moorland on the outskirts of town.

"What makes you think I couldn't?" she demanded, and to her own surprise, adding, daringly, "I would hardly have applied for the position if I thought for one moment I wasn't capable of handling it, Mr Prentice."

He shrugged. "In the past, we have had the oddest kind of females apply for positions in the house and as my secretary. I don't know why you should feel I should trust my niece to your care. Perhaps you would be good enough to tell me."

Now, completely unnerved by his manner, Kerri sat holding her breath, while his exasperating deep chuckle rasped across her nerves.

"I can see you cannot think of one cohesive answer to my questions, Miss Matheson. You've come to apply for a job as companion to a young girl, but you haven't the slightest experience in this type of work. Since leaving school you have dealt with members of the public, admittedly, but in a very different sphere. You expect, I suppose, my niece to behave and let you get your bearings, as it were, at your leisure."

Again the deep chuckle echoed through the room. "You don't know my niece! Why do you suppose I need someone to keep an eye on her? She's at an age when she is swayed by her emotions and she doesn't take too kindly to orders. Besides which, you don't look all that older than Jane herself. *Do* you really think you would be able to control her, Miss Matheson?"

"Are you trying to put me off, Mr Prentice?" Kerri's glare was quite fierce.

"Not at all, Miss Matheson. I'm just warning you what to expect."

There was silence for a moment, then he said, "Well, knowing all that, would you still be prepared to drop everything and come with us to Lessane? We leave the day after tomorrow."

"I think I could be ready," she managed at last.

Before she had time to comment further, he had rapped out. "I don't want you to *think*. I want you to be sure."

"I'm sure," she said, matching his crisp tones with her own.

"Well, quite frankly, I'm not. As a chaperon to my niece you would only add to my problems. You're much too young, for a start. I need someone older, more responsible. Why, you could barely have left school yourself not all that long ago."

Kerri heard his words with a sinking of her heart. He had made no secret of his scorn from the moment he had laid eyes on her. Now, gazing into the glittering grey eyes and the ominous scowl, she couldn't honestly say she was sorry at the idea of not having him for a boss. He'd been playing a cat-and-mouse game with her, it seemed. No, definitely, now that she had met him, the position had lost much of its former enchantment.

She said, gathering up her handbag and gloves, in preparation for leaving, "Well, that seems to be that, doesn't it? I'm sorry you had to waste your precious time interviewing me, Mr Prentice. Maybe the next applicant will be more promising."

There was a hint of spite in her words that was not lost on him.

He chose to ignore it, however, saying as he rose, "So far, they have all been impossible." His voice was full of contempt. "It was a last gamble, trying just one more time. It seems now I will have to make do with the one woman who applied who seemed acceptable."

His frown was ominous. "She is perhaps older than I envisaged, but I've wasted enough time as it is on this project."

He turned to the bell pull, tugging at it with irritation, and a moment later, the forbidding housekeeper appeared. She held open the door for Kerri, gazing at her with thinly veiled contempt, and just before she left she heard the tall man say, "I hope you find something to your satisfaction, Miss Matheson. Kate will see you to the taxi. Now, if you'll excuse me . . . "

He turned away, going to the big desk

before the window and seating himself at it, as though weary of the whole business.

Kerri's legs trembled as she walked through the hall to the front door and climbed back into the waiting taxi. The housekeeper stood in the open doorway, her mouth set in contemptuous lines, a wary, thoughtful look in her eyes.

Oh, well, you can't win 'em all, as her brother was fond of saying. Even so, her cheeks flamed in anger as she instructed the taxi-driver to take her back the way they had come. Once driving through the lovely countryside, though, she wasted no time in regrets, telling herself that the man would have been impossible to work for, anyway. Imagine seeing *him* every day, even in a paradise like Lessane?

He would truly be the serpent in the Garden of Eden!

Really, she should consider herself lucky that he *had* thought her too young and not responsible enough for the job.

She discovered that the housekeeper had paid the taxi-driver, for when she reached her home he smiled and assured her everything was 'fixed'.

In the kitchen she found her mother peeling potatoes for lunch. She wiped her hands on a cloth and smiled at Kerri, asking how she'd got on.

Kerri threw her handbag on to the kitchen table and helped herself to an apple from the woven cane basket in the centre of the bright red cloth.

She said, small teeth biting into it viciously, "Let's just say it was a complete waste of time. He thought I was too young."

Her mother tut-tutted with her tongue, looking at her with sympathy.

"What a shame! A summer spent in that place would have done you the world of good, too. Let's face it, Kerri, you've been awfully touchy lately. Don't you think a good tonic from Dr Macleod would be the answer?"

Kerri sighed. The solution, as far as she was concerned, didn't lie in the bottle of sweet-tasting medicine prescribed by the old doctor who had delivered her and her brother and who had seen them safely through measles and chickenpox and all the other ailments of childhood.

She didn't *know* the answer.

"Anyway," went on her mother, turning back to the half-peeled potatoes in the kitchen sink, "I'm sure you'll have no trouble finding something suitable. A girl like you, Kerri, with your nice manners . . . "

She left it at that and Kerri turned away, picked up her handbag and went to her bedroom. The morning's ordeal had soured her for other interviews and she certainly didn't wish to repeat the experience, not too soon, anyway.

She'd give it another few days before applying for another job, even if it meant having to accept one in another travel agency.

2

THE following day she caught the bus into town, and spent the afternoon strolling round the shops. In one of the department stores she bumped into a friend, a girl whom she had known since schooldays and whose wedding she had attended just over a year ago.

The girl was heavily pregnant and accepted with delight Kerri's suggestion that they have tea together. They sat in the bay window of the old-fashioned café, at first discussing old times, then Kerri listening with amusement to the girl talking about her coming baby, about the names she and her husband had decided upon.

"Tom thinks Craig is nice," she said, patting her tummy complacently, "but personally I like Grant."

Kerri laughed. "What if it's a girl?" she suggested. "It *can* happen, you know."

The girl made a grimace. "Oh, well,

I suppose then we'd have to change our minds. But Tom is convinced it's going to be a boy. He's dying to teach him to play rugby."

Now, getting off the bus alone and walking home through the soft spring twilight Kerri felt vague longings stirring inside her. Longings she couldn't explain. She found herself humming a catchy tune she'd heard recently on television, in one of the old movies — "I'm as restless as a willow in a wind storm . . . "and stepped through the front door to find her mother waiting in the hall, a look of flushed excitement on her face.

"Oh, Kerri, there was a phone call for you. A Mr Prentice. He said you were to call back just as soon as you get home. He said it was important."

For a long moment Kerri hesitated, wondering if she should call the offensive young man, and then thinking that if she didn't might she not regret it.

What on earth could he want her for! Surely he hadn't changed his mind again? Too confused to think properly, before she had time to make comment on this latest development, her mother went on, eagerly, "He sounded very pleasant, Kerri, and very worried. Said he was sorry he had to mess you about like this but that he really *must* speak to you, and as soon as possible."

Kerri sighed. For several minutes she debated on the advisability of whether to call or to ignore it. Her strict upbringing impelled her not to ignore it. At the same time her head warned her to be cautious. Don't be hasty, it said. The man is impossible. How ever could her mother have imagined he sounded pleasant! Perhaps he was one of those people who can turn charm on and off like a tap, especially to older women, she thought.

Well, that cut no ice with her. Let him keep his charm. She would telephone him, as requested, hear what he had to say, then, if he was offering her the job, inform him politely but firmly that she was no longer interested.

Hurrying to the phone, she dialled his number, which her mother had scribbled on a pad near the phone, for she would never have recalled it otherwise, and waited for the faint ringing to cease.

31

The housekeeper's harsh voice answered, and Kerri said, "This is Miss Matheson speaking. May I speak to Mr Prentice, please?"

There was a short silence, as though the woman debated on the expediency of such an action. Then she said, "Very well. I'll call him."

Before she had time to collect her thoughts, or decide how she should begin, the deep voice rasped in her ear, "Dominic Prentice speaking. Is that Miss Matheson?"

"Eh — yes." Her mouth went dry so that her answer came out as a croak. She called herself all kinds of a fool but was unable to control the quick leaping of her pulse at the sound of his voice.

"Good. I've decided I need you after all. Pack your things and take a taxi so that you will be here early on the morning of the 20th. Today is the 18th, so it will give you very little time to get ready. Bring everything you think you will need, for there won't be time to do any shopping. My niece will have to purchase anything she is short of on the island. We will pick her up on the way to the airport."

Kerri gasped. So cool, so calm! Expecting everyone to jump to his bidding! She said, trying to make her voice steadier than it really was, "I take it, Mr Prentice, you are offering me the job. What happened to that other applicant, the one who was much more suitable?" If he noted the faint sarcasm in her voice he didn't show it. His sigh over the humming wires was clearly audible. "Do you, or do you not, still want the position, Miss Matheson? Because, if you have changed your mind, one of the more irritating requisites of your sex, I would like to know. Otherwise, kindly do as I say. If you must know, the other applicant, a Miss Graham and infinitely more suitable than you will ever be, Miss Matheson, met with a slight accident when crossing the street and is in hospital. Not serious but enough to cancel out any hopes I had of engaging her for my niece."

"I'm sorry. That she was involved in an accident, I mean."

The quick sympathy in Kerri's voice was not lost on him, although his tone was still caustic when he answered, dryly, "Your sympathy does you credit, Miss Matheson. Can I take it, then, that you will be here on the morning of the 20th?"

To her surprise — and slight disgust when she thought about it later — Kerri heard herself saying, "Yes, Mr Prentice, you can depend on me being there."

She hung up, unable to believe she had actually allowed herself to fall in with this overbearing man's instructions. The colossal conceit of him!

Without giving her proper consideration at the interview he had told her she was too young, not 'responsible' enough, and now, out of the blue, without any 'please' or 'thank you', he had snapped his fingers and expected her to come running.

And she had accepted, tamely, spinelessly, as though she had no will of her own. It was only later, as she sat watching television with her family, her thoughts far away from the humdrum play about lorry-drivers and their 'pick-ups', that the full realisation of what she had done came to her. Curiously, it brought with it a sense of achievement.

Now that she had had time to become used to the idea, she could hardly believe her luck.

Even though the colossal arrogance of the man still irked her, the thought of the next few months more than made up for it, and, after all, surely she wouldn't have to see all that much of him, her attention being concentrated mainly on his niece. Jane. Aged sixteen.

What would the girl be like? she wondered. Friendly, confiding, or conceited and prickly, like her uncle? She hoped not. Kerri got on with most people, and children and dogs adored her; her mother often remarked that that was a sign of one's good character if animals like you . . .

Oh, well, no use worrying about it now, causing her mind to whirl like leaves caught in an autumn gale. Time to discover the nature and character of the girl who was to be her charge when she met her. Then she thought; salary hadn't been mentioned. He was so sure of himself that she supposed he thought she would jump at the job regardless of what he offered.

Her sleep was uneasy and the morning she was to leave she awoke with the beginnings of a headache. While packing the night before she had thought that she still didn't know what had possessed her to accept so tamely.

★ ★ ★

The long sleek limousine that they had travelled in slid to a halt in front of the red brick building that was Jane's school. The main house was covered in pale green tendrils of Virginia creeper and Kerri found herself watching the wide, arched doorway with some trepidation in which was mixed anxiety. Would the girl like her? It was so important that she did. What if they couldn't stand each other, if all the faults of her uncle had come out again in her? Kerri's mouth twisted. Oh, no, she didn't think she could stand that if that proved the case, paradise island with its blue lagoon or not. That would be *too* much for any one girl to bear.

They would be in each other's company quite a lot, and it would be much more pleasant if they got on well together.

Anyway, hadn't Mr Prentice mentioned the book on which he would be working? In all probability that would keep him busy and she would have time to get to know the girl without too much interference on his part. Too much of his company she didn't think she could take. A man like that one took in small doses, she thought. *Very* small doses, indeed!

She thought of him as she had stepped from the taxi earlier that morning. He had come forward to meet her, glanced down at her suitcases and called to the uniformed chauffeur to take them from the taxi-driver. Suddenly excrutiatingly self-conscious of the shrewed look he directed at her, she flushed as he murmured, "So you made it, then?"

She met his eyes. "Of course! Didn't you think I would?"

He shrugged. "I'm experienced enough to know women are seldom on time for an appointment. It's rather refreshing to find one who is."

He sounded so exasperated at that moment that Kerri wondered about the woman responsible for those bitter thoughts. Someone he had loved? Someone who had let him down?

Odd, she didn't even know if he was married . . . But of course he wasn't. If there was a wife somewhere, surely there would be no *need* for a companion for his niece . . . Unless the wife preferred the gaiety and bright lights of London to the utter solitude of some Pacific island. . . .

Watching the chauffeur place her luggage in the large boot, he turned to her and asked, "Is this the lot?"

Again Kerri felt her cheeks flushing. "I — I hadn't much to pack. I thought I might buy some light cotton things once we're settled on the island."

"Good idea. No doubt Jane will need some extra things too. The school uniform she is forced to wear is hideous and I know she'll be delighted for any excuse to spend money." He grinned down at her, an involuntary gleam of amusement in his eyes. "Not that, where my niece is concerned, an excuse is needed. She has, as I mentioned before, very decided ideas on what she wants, and, where my brother is concerned, invariably *gets* and I rely on you to resist her demands. And, believe me, that is what they will be — demands. If her mother were still alive, no doubt she . . . ”

He broke off, as though aware of the sudden sharpened interest in Kerri's eyes. So, she thought, the girl's mother *was* dead! Poor child! Fancy having to rely on a father who was far more interested in the ruins of ancient civilisations, plus an uncle who was just as stuffy, for comfort and understanding in your years of adolescence.

“I hope she will like me,” she suggested, a little timidly.

“That's beside the point.” His tone was sarcastic again. “It's more important that you can control her. Oh, not that I expect you to be able to do that, not immediately, that is,” seeing the doubt on her face. “But I have no hesitation in thinking that in a few days you will find a way. Women usually do get what they want.”

There it was again, she thought. That undercurrent of bitterness. Someone in the past had definitely left a scar on his emotions that was taking a long time to heal. Some woman . . . ?

She set her mouth determinedly. Well, she would show him that not all women were the same. That she wasn't to be intimidated by his surly manner, and that she would see this thing through whatever the consequences. And, to be perfectly honest with herself, wasn't this just what she had been looking for? A job that was different, that took her out of an everyday world that was getting increasingly more tedious?

In the long drive to the school, she sat with her face turned away, watching the countryside through which they drove. Finally, so many questions were chasing one another around in her mind, that she turned to him to say, hesitantly, "Perhaps if I could ask a few questions . . . ?"

His look was impatient. "Very well. What exactly would you like to know?"

"Well, to begin with, an idea of your niece's daily routine so that I know roughly what she'll be expecting to do."

"That isn't really necessary," he said. "You're not expected to plan her day for her, she's perfectly capable of doing that for herself. Your job will be to watch her, to know at all times where she is."

"Why?"

The question seemed to irritate him. "Because that is what I am paying you for," he said succinctly, and the remark seemed to end that part of the conversation.

41

3

NOW, sitting in the comfortable limousine, waiting for the girl and her uncle, who had disappeared inside the heavy front door of the school, to 'Rake her out', as, with some impatience, he'd put it, she watched eagerly, if a little apprehensively, for them to appear.

When they did, the girl, tall, slim, looking fragile against her tall, broad-shouldered uncle, threw out her arms and lifted her face to the sun, as though gaining freedom for the first time in many months. Kerri found herself examining with some misgiving the small, piquant features and long shining blonde hair, so fair as to be almost silver. She heard her say as they reached the car and the chauffeur held open the door, "Gosh, Dominic, I seem to have been waiting simply *ages*. What took you so long? I was beginning to think you'd changed your mind and I would have to stay in that concentration camp with old Bogy as my only companion, for the rest of the summer."

Her uncle settled her next to Kerri, then climbed in himself. His voice was a little clipped as he said, reprovingly, "I don't think you should talk like that about your headmistress. Miss Boguy is an extremely competent woman and you should be proud that she takes so much interest in your well-being. And, young lady, St Clare's is hardly a 'concentration camp'. Your father chose it as one of the most exclusive girls' schools in the country. Now," leaning forward slightly so that he could see Kerri's expression as he introduced them, "This is Miss Matheson. She will be keeping an eye on you while we are on Lessane."

The girl pouted, looking mutinous. "For heaven's *sake*, Dominic! I don't *need* anyone to 'keep an eye on me', as you so joyfully put it. I'm turned sixteen. You seem to forget that. Hardly a babe anymore. I'm quite capable of looking after myself . . ."

His mouth quirked. "That remains to be seen. Don't imagine for one moment, young lady, that I'm looking forward to having you with me for the whole summer. Far from it. I had hoped to be able to get on with some serious writing, but it seems my hopes were to be dashed. Notwithstanding all that, Miss Matheson will be with us and I trust there will be no attempt, on your part, to make her life a misery."

Inwardly recoiling at the direction Dominic Prentice's welcome to his niece was taking, Kerri found herself raked by a pair of tawny brown eyes that held no trace of warmth or friendliness. Not even liking. The almost fully developed figure beneath the school uniform, a dark, olive-green gymslip and cream flannel blouse, was held stiffly, as though to relax for a moment might lower her defences and that she had no intention of doing.

Kerri felt dismay overtake her. This girl was going to be difficult! But hadn't Mr Prentice warned her of that. Hadn't he said, "My niece doesn't take kindly to orders . . . " and "It isn't important that she should like you, only that you can control her."

Well, to start with there would be no

44

doubt as to this girl's likes and dislikes. But there was the summer ahead of them; Lessane golden beaches fringed by a warm blue sea, days spent swimming and sunbathing and if those conditions weren't right for forming friendships, then Kerri didn't know what was.

She smiled at the girl and said pleasant, "Hello Jane. It's going to be fun, isn't it? I've never been to that part of the world before, although I've done some travelling on the Continent. I love Greece . . ."

Ignoring her uncle's look of warning, the girl gave a slight smile, her lips hardly twitching, and replied, "I've been with my father to most of those places. Greece is one big bore. Digs where my father spends most of his day — you know what 'digs' are, I suppose? Excavations of ancient places. My father pays more attention to the dead than to the living . . ."

"Jane!" Dominic Prentice's voice held censure. "I'm sure Miss Matheson has no desire to listen to your grievances of past holidays with your father. Archaeology is your father's life and it isn't for us to complain because of the interest he takes in it."

"No, we mustn't complain, must we? Even though my mother would still have been alive today if you had both taken more interest in her feelings . . . "

The bitterness of the remark put Kerri off her stroke a little. Still, if what the girl said was true, then Jane's attitude wasn't entirely unexpected. A small silence had fallen over the interior of the smoothly moving car, and she forced herself to say, lightly, "How long does the flight take? Is it direct or will we have to go via somewhere else?"

The small agency where she had worked had never handled or had even had a request for travel to the island of Lesanne.

Aware that she was trying to break the feeling of tension that had erupted with Jane's remarks about her father, Dominic smiled slightly, answering pleasantly enough, "We go by Pan Am. Lessane, in case you didn't know, is one of a group of over three hundred mainly volcanic islands in the Pacific Ocean. We fly to Roa. From there we take

46

another, smaller plane to Lessane. The airport on the island is not very big and can only handle light planes."

Kerri glowed. "It sounds fascinating," she breathed, rapturously.

Jane shrugged. "It sounds boring. I've been there before with Dominic and all these places are the same, except for the people." She turned her head to look at her uncle, adding, "Why on earth couldn't you have chosen some other place, Dominic, to write your silly book? Somewhere like Paris or San Francisco?"

"May I remind you that I need peace and a certain amount of solitude to write *any*thing? Paris or San Francisco would hardly have given me that. Besides, Lessane is ideal for a girl of your age. Do you the world of good."

"Yes," said Kerri eagerly. "The very idea of swimming every day and all that sun makes my mouth water."

Jane caught her eye. "Well," she murmured, "it takes all sorts, I suppose." She gave a little toss of her head, as though she was challenging comment. Kerri had more sense than to make any. She realised she would have to take it slowly with this girl, ignoring her mocking remarks, making a show of complete understanding no matter what her private feelings were.

Again she wondered if she had done the right thing in accepting the position of looking after Jane for the summer. Then her natural sympathy took over. She reminded herself it couldn't have been much fun for the girl, her mother dead — under what tragic circumstances, Kerri wondered — and her father far more interested in his work than his young daughter; abandoned to the impersonal life of a boarding-school for most of the year.

Behind those lovely but cold brown eyes there might well be an aching loneliness. Thinking of her own emotional mother, her father and brother, Neil, even if at times he did tease the life out of her, Kerri felt almost ashamed of her own closely knit family.

She sat keyed up in the atmosphere of the car. Jane continued to stare out of the window and as Mr Prentice showed no inclination to talk Kerri did the same, leaning back against the soft leather upholstery and letting herself enjoy the scenery through which they were passing.

All the same, she resolved to make the girl's summer in Lessane as happy as she could.

The ride to the airport seemed interminable. She began to fidget, disconcerted at having Dominic Prentice so close, acutely aware of the dark hair curling about his ears and the strong clean-shaven jaw. Soon the traffic of the city was left behind and they came on to the fast-moving motorway leading to the airport.

Kerri felt jaded already, having had such an early start, hardly any breakfast, and their journey had only just began. She saw planes in the distance and her interest perked up. She loved flying, travelling in any form, and in the bustle and activity of the departure lounge she was soon her old self again. On the other hand, Jane seemed not interested in anything, not even the sheaf of glossy magazines her uncle had purchased for her to read on the flight. She gave Kerri the impression that the whole thing was one big bore — the way she had described past summers in Greece with her father.

They waited while the luggage was weighed. Then the tickets had to be checked. There seemed so much to do, so much to take care of, that Kerri felt the muscles at the base of her neck beginning to tighten, a heavy throbbing commence over her eyes.

When at last it seemed all the formalities had been taken care of, Dominic ushered them along the passage-way to the entrance of the huge plane. Jane indicated that Kerri could have the seat near the window and once settled they watched as the air hostess demonstrated the way to wear a life-jacket.

Kerry glanced surreptitiously at her neighbours, across the magazine that Jane had already opened, wondering if they were the only passengers on this huge flying machine that were travelling halfway across the world. As the engines gradually increased their power, she held her breath. It was an involuntary gesture, something she had never been able to control. London dropped away and gradually she forced herself to relax.

All about them people were settling down, lighting cigarettes now that the flashing red sign had disappeared, all apparently at ease, all apparently slightly bored; not one, it seemed, conscious of the speed with which England was slipping away beneath them.

She wondered again where they were all going, and why, and if any of them had a summer ahead of them as interesting, as challenging as the one she faced. The drone of the engines became soporific, drowsy, and she tried to take an interest in one of the magazines Dominic had bought for them, but nothing registered on her weary senses. Her eyes would insist on closing and some of her lassitude must have transferred itself to Jane, for she looked across at her, frowning, enquiring, "Are you all right? You don't get air-sick or anything ghastly like that, do you?"

Kerri gave a soft laugh, shaking her head. "No, nothing like that, thank goodness. It's just that I was up so early this morning and didn't bother with breakfast — your uncle wanted an early start, and I guess it's just catching up on me."

Jane considered her for a moment, then said, "Well, why don't you try to sleep, then? You're not going to be needed for the next few hours, are you? I mean, to spy on me?"

Kerri felt her cheeks flush. "You're uncle didn't engage me to *spy* on you, Jane, no matter what you might think to the contrary . . ."

The girl rustled the pages of her magazine, lowering her eyes from Kerri's troubled stare. "Is that what he told you? We mustn't believe all we're told, you know. Or so the eminent headmistress of St Clare's is always trying to impress upon us."

Searching for an answer and not finding one that didn't sound impertinent, Kerri pursed her lips and turned her head away to gaze out of the window beside her.

Blue skies partly covered with fleeting white clouds, the wing of the plane glinting silver just below her window. Perhaps this summer wasn't going to be as wonderful as she had envisaged, but at least she would endeavour to keep her temper, to control the impulse to answer back, both to this petulant schoolgirl and her arrogant uncle.

And surely the warm blue seas and the sunshine would more than make up for any disagreeableness she might have to contend with.

The flight seemed endless. Meals were served, then after another doze from which she awoke feeling stiff with her headache worse, they landed at Malso Airport. Their wait to transfer to a smaller plane was brief and within an hour they were on their way again. This journey was much shorter and it seemed hardly any time at all before the plane was circling, dipping one wing beyond which Kerri could see nothing but water. Then it straightened out and she gasped in delight.

Palm trees, bent to the trade winds, guarded silver white beaches, while the water, in varying shades of turquoise, aquamarine and deep purple, depending on depth, plucked lazily at its white fringes. About half a mile out white water broke over a reef of coral.

Kerri's heart palpitated with excitement;

the ground came rushing up to meet them, there was a bump of wheels touching, and palm trees and sand rushed by, an exotic frieze that seemed never to stop.

Just when she was sure they would overshoot the small island and so have to make the descent again the engines slowed and they came to a rest beside a small white building.

4

JANE folded her magazine, stretched, yawned and said, "Oh, well, I suppose if you must survive the next few months without actually *dying* of boredom, I suppose we must. Come on, Miss Matheson, let's see what we make of the place."

Kerri's eyes flew towards Dominic Prentice, who had also risen, reaching for his briefcase from the rack above their heads. His cool gaze met hers, and he smiled. "Ready, girls? All right, come on. No time for dawdling. We've still a long way to go."

Reading the question in her eyes, Jane said, "He means to the house, clear across to the other side of the island. A drag! The roads are atrocious, if you can call them roads."

Kerri smiled, hearing the girl's uncle say, reprovingly, "Jane! Stop moaning and try to enjoy yourself. Or, at least, if you find that impossible to do, kindly allow others to do so. Miss Matheson must have heard enough of your grievances to last her the rest of the summer."

Kerri felt she could hardly say it aloud, but she altogether agreed with him, for once. The girl's attitude of utter and desolate boredom was depressing and she wondered how long she would be able to endure it without showing signs of strain. And that would never do. Dominic Prentice was paying her to be a congenial companion to his niece, and no matter what she privately felt, or how much she agreed with his sentiments about Jane's attitude, she must be careful never to show her real feelings.

But, she thought, wryly, it wasn't going to be easy!

Any resentment that was building up inside her, and to be sure there was plenty of that, must be carefully concealed. She thought of the girls she knew, girls who could barely afford a holiday at all, never mind on a tropical paradise in the Pacific, who would gladly give their eyes for such an opportunity. Although that would rather defeat the object . . .

She followed the other two along the

aisle, down the steps on to a softly melting tarmac, for the heat was fierce, and across to the airport buildings. The glare of the sun made her head spin and she thought the first thing she must do was buy herself a large pair of dark glasses, also a broad-brimmed hat . . .

As she walked, hurrying after the tall, broad-shouldered man and the young girl, she felt her legs trembling beneath her. There was a funny hissing sound in her ears and though she tried to walk straight she felt herself swaying. The sun became a brilliant dazzle before her eyes and without a sound, before Dominic or his niece or indeed any of the passengers on the small plane was aware of it, she crumpled to the ground and fainted dead away.

Kerri came round to find herself lying on one of the leather-covered settees in the airport lounge. Jane was holding a glass of water, her lips screwed up with distaste at the small knot of people, of all colours and nationalities, who stood staring at them.

Dominic bent over her, the scowl on his face plain in his concern for the delay her mishap was causing them.

Not, she thought, for any regards for her . . .

"Are you all right?" His voice was gruff, showing scant sympathy. "Good Lord, girl, you gave us the fright of our lives. One minute you're following us from the aircraft, the next keeling over on the tarmac . . . "

One or two people in the small crowd murmured sympathetically, but he ignored them. "Think you can manage the rest of the journey?" he went on, his voice almost harsh.

She wouldn't, for the life of her, give him the satisfaction of thinking she couldn't. She managed to sit up, pushing his hand away, and said, "Of course. I'm fine now. Sorry I did that — I don't really know what happened."

Someone in the crowd murmured, "The sun, that's what it is. If you're not used to it it can play havoc with you . . . "

Feeling his arm placed beneath her shoulders, assisting her to her feet, Kerri gave Dominic a washed-out smile as he muttered, "Here, hang on to me.

Although, in future, Miss Matheson, I would appreciate it if you arranged your fainting spells at more convenient moments."

There was an underlying note of irritation in his voice that made her flush. Testily, she began, "If you think for one moment . . . " then caught herself in time, biting her lip to stop the flow of angry words.

Really, he was insufferable! Did he think she had done it on purpose, fainted dead away on the hot, sticky tarmac, in front of all those strangers, just to annoy him?

She heard Jane's voice in the background. "Are you sure you're feeling better?" Kerri saw her look round at the crowd who were now beginning to drift away. "Because, if you are, we should move. I mean, I felt so — so *embarrassed*, everyone looking at us like that."

Kerri took a deep breath and swung her legs to the floor. They still felt trembly but she was sure she could manage. *Anything*, to spare this rather scornful man and his niece further embarrassment, no matter what she herself felt.

All the same, it felt decidedly odd walking with one arm of her irate employer about her. He seemed to sense her hesitation and went slowly, crossing the floor of the airport lounge to the various authorities who waited, and then assisting her to the large car that was parked outside.

As Jane had said, they had almost to cross the entire length of the island before they came to the large white house built practically on to the beach.

A long, low, bungalow-type residence where palm trees bent their feathery heads above the green-tiled roof and only a low wall separated it from the beach proper.

One would hear the murmur of the ocean from the time one opened one's eyes in the morning until closing them at night, Kerri thought. The sharp, tangy salt of the water was heavy in one's nostrils, blending with the sweetly smelling tropical flowers that grew everywhere. Already she was feeling her old self again, the girl who had answered that advertisement in the first place.

A wide terrace faced the sea from the back of the house and huge glass doors, sliding back on oiled runners, opened on to it. There was a huge lounge with comfortable-looking settees and large easy chairs, a stereo, and a piano in one corner, and, to Kerri's surprise in such a setting of tropical splendour, a large fireplace built of natural stone.

An arrangement of dried grasses and flowers stood in a copper jug in the empty grate, but Kerri could imagine it on a wild, stormy night, the wind fierce, the sea raging against the encircling reef. Here, they would be warm and safe, the room cosy, the cherry-red coals of the fire gleaming . . .

She smiled. *Did* islands in this latitude ever experience such weather? Somehow she doubted it. Although the world would be a tame place without seasons, she thought. Then there would be a sameness that was unnatural, the same thing, day in, day out. . . .

But there was no more time to take in everything. Servants, brown-skinned and smiling, came hurrying forward and together with Jane and her uncle Kerri followed them along passages, stopping first at the door of Jane's room.

The girl tossed an indifferent glance over the luxurious furnishings, while her uncle asked, "Is anything wrong? You know you prefer this room to all the others. But if you would like to change, I will give instructions."

Jane shook her head. "No. I suppose if I'm forced to spend the summer in this dump, this will do as well as anything."

Dominic sighed. He looked at her as one would a small child. A very much spoiled child, thought Kerri. Leaving the girl to her sulking, she went along with the maid and was shown to her own room. Although the furniture was heavy and old-fashioned, made of dark wood that looked very old, somehow the large square bed, with its white hangings, suited the surroundings. She saw that she had been given an adjoining bathroom and that the long windows opened, like the lounge, on to the terrace.

But there was no time to take in everything. After a quick wash and change, she opened her door and drifted out into the passage. She felt much cooler and fresher, the white polyester gown she had chosen simple yet elegant.

She tapped on Jane's bedroom door and at the girl's answering, "Oh, who is it?" in a peevish voice, she opened it and went in.

Jane stood in her slip, a plain white cotton one and was gazing at herself in the long mirror of the dressing-table. Turning to Kerri, she grimaced and said, "Thank heavens I'll be able to discard this for a while. Did you ever see anything so hideous? Old Bogy insists on the girls 'wearing plain simple undergarments'," and her voice took on a high falsetto note that Kerri imagined was supposed to resemble the inestimable Miss Boguy.

The girl began to pull the slip over her head, not waiting or seeming to expect a reply from Kerri, and flung the offending garment on to the floor. She turned back to the dressing-table and started to brush her hair with a vigour that made Kerri smile. Bending over, Kerri picked up the discarded slip and hung it neatly over the bedrail.

"It isn't exactly anything to get excited about, I'll admit," she smiled. "But modest and practical and no doubt very suitable for the life you lead."

Jane sniffed. "Modest! You can say that again! Oh, to get into something really glam, that doesn't have to be modest! And to think I've brought hardly anything with me." She went over to the opened suitcase lying on the bed, and began to rummage in the pile of once neatly folded things there with impatient haste, finally settling on a shocking pink kaftan with a design in darker pink of large swirls all over it.

Jane giggled. "I bought this last year in Morocco when I was there with Daddy. Dominic hasn't seen it yet. Do you think he'll like it?"

She twisted and turned before the long mirror, looking over her shoulder to see herself from all angles. The kaftan made her look like a little girl dressed up in her mother's clothes.

Dominic obviously thought the same when they joined him later in the large lounge. The doors had been pushed back and the view of the beach, with its fringe of palms and beyond that the vivid blueness of the ocean, was breathtaking.

Dominic rose to his feet as they entered. Kerri saw he was still in his dark suit and she wondered how he managed to look so cool and relaxed all the time. The look he gave his niece was penetrating, taking in the rather exotic-looking kaftan and the way she had done her hair; drawn up from her face into a sort of topknot high on her small head. It made her look years older and Kerri couldn't really blame him when, making no attempt to be tactful, he said, "Good God! Whatever have you done to yourself, child? You look like something out of a Tennessee Williams play. Go and change and be quick about it. God knows what your father would say if he could see you now."

Jane pouted, but before she could say anything, turning towards Kerri, he went on, curtly, "I can see I had better brief you on your duties, after all, Miss Matheson, included in which is an effort to keep my niece looking neat and tidy at all times."

Kerri felt her face go pink and her ears burned with embarrassment.

"Mr Prentice . . . " she began, but

he wasn't listening. He resumed his seat by the open doors and picked up the newspaper he had been reading on their arrival. Without taking his eyes from the newsprint, he murmured, "Please go and see that my niece changes immediately. I believe the servants are waiting to serve a meal and we don't want to keep them waiting any longer."

Thinking wryly that she hadn't done a very good job of managing the girl, Kerri followed her out of the room and along the passage, back to the bedroom. Mutinously, Jane flung off the offending kaftan, leaving it to lie in a small heap on the carpet, before slipping on a simple cotton dress in pale blue, which Kerri told her looked very becoming, feeling a bit like her own mother as she did.

"The old bear!" the girl muttered sulkily. "I can see we're going to have a whale of a time with him in *that* mood."

"Well, then," answered Kerri, making an effort to keep her voice soothing, "don't let's antagonise him then, shall we? I mean, it isn't going to help if you insist on doing things that you know will make him mad."

She bent to pick up the kaftan from the floor. "Let's face it, Jane, it isn't really a suitable gown for a young girl to wear, is it?"

The girl's scowl deepened. "Suitable! How I detest that word. It is one of old Bogy's favourite expressions. Suitable this and suitable that. I don't think I'll ever wear a suitable thing, after this, in my whole life."

Kerri smiled and accompanied her back to the lounge. It was obvious, she thought, when at one time during the meal, she caught Dominic's stern grey gaze, that she was going to have to do better in future.

5

AFTERWARDS Dominic led them on to the terrace facing the ocean, and they drank coffee from tiny blue and gold cups. It was delicious, and Kerri thought he must employ an excellent cook, for indeed the whole meal had been an epicure's delight.

Dusk came early in these climes and almost before they knew it darkness had settled over the ocean and surrounding gardens. An amber-coloured lamp was switched on above their heads, illuminating the pale silver hair of Jane and the stern, clear-cut profile of Dominic Prentice as he poured brandy from a cut-glass decanter a servant had placed at his side on a silver tray.

He lifted his glass to Kerri, brows raised questioningly, but she shook her head. Jane, she noticed, hadn't even been consulted. Swirling the clear golden liquid round in the large globe-shaped glass, he looked at the two girls, his mouth twitching almost involuntarily at the scowl of discontent that still lingered on his niece's face.

"For heaven's sake, Jane, don't sulk. You still have plenty to keep you occupied." His voice was brisk, detached almost. "The house has its own private stretch of beach, and there aren't many days when you won't be able to swim or sunbathe. I'll leave instructions for Morello to drive you into town if you feel like shopping."

His gaze switched to Kerri. "There are a few good shops, a couple of bazaars which you should find interesting, and if you become *too* bored with all this," waving one hand negligently to indicate their surroundings, "there is the Hotel Topaze. It boasts a very good restaurant, if you feel like popping in for tea some time, a swimming-pool and tennis courts, also a nightclub, but that's something we'll stay clear of."

He drained his glass and without waiting, or indeed seeming to expect, a reply from either of the girls, he said briskly, "Well, that's it for today. I think an early night is indicated, especially after that long journey and Miss Matheson's little fainting episode. By the way," giving Kerri a look that was too preoccupied to be sincere, "how are you feeling now? I must say that fainting spell of yours at the airport was totally unexpected." His mouth twisted sardonically. "I didn't think young ladies did that any more."

Without waiting for Kerri's answer — not that she *had* an answer — he added easily, if a little pompously, "You will find it useful to remember, Miss Matheson, that the sun can be an enemy as well as a friend. For instance, it's always wise to rest after a meal in these parts, and especially never go swimming directly after one. Up to mid-morning or late afternoon is the best time, you'll find."

Kerri nodded meekly and followed a rebellious Jane back along the passage to their rooms. She had got the feeling that Dominic Prentice had every intention of treating her like a child, in spite of her status in the household.

All right, he paid her salary and if he wanted to act stuffy and overbearing that was his privilege. But she couldn't help wondering what he would be like if he allowed himself to ease up just a bit, to laugh and take pleasure in their lovely surroundings.

It was almost eight o'clock the following morning when she woke and got out of bed to throw open the curtains to the sun. A plump maid beamed as she brought in her morning tea, and sipping this Kerri leaned back on the pillows while she planned their morning, although she knew she would have to consult Jane before she could make any definite plans.

She grimaced, wondering if she would have to ask Dominic Prentice's permission, too, and prayed that she wouldn't. Surely the very reason he had hired her was to keep the girl, as far as possible, out from under his feet? Hadn't he admitted as much on their first meeting, so he really couldn't blame her if she went ahead with plans of her own.

To Kerri's relief there was no sign of Dominic when she made her way on to the cool terrace where the maid had informed her on fine mornings breakfast was always served. The ocean looked very blue and inviting and she thought a few hours spent floating in its inviting waters would be sheer heaven.

Jane joined her at the table a short time later and for the first time her face lit up with something like enthusiasm when Kerri sounded her out about a morning spent swimming and sunbathing.

Her voice took on an eager tone and Kerri was thankful that the boredom of yesterday was forgotten. She hurried with her breakfast and flew back to her room, reappearing in a pale pink bikini and a matching towel drape. Kerri's own costume was a white one-piece that showed off her figure to perfection.

It was a relief to know that they were going to be on their own, and after a while Jane unfroze with almost gay abandon. The two girls laughed and talked to each other as they played in the warm surf.

"Have you ever done any surfing?" she asked Kerri at one time as they sat with long slim legs stretched out before them on the fine sand.

Kerri shook her head. "No. Somehow

just looking at the people doing it makes me nervous."

Jane looked thoughtful. "I've always wanted to, but Daddy never really liked the idea. He's very protective, you know. *Too* protective at times, I think."

Kerri laughed. "With that hair and those eyes, my girl, your father is going to *have* to be protective in a few years' time."

"Really!" It might have been a different girl, sitting on the sand, gazing at Kerri so attentively. "Do you really think so, Kerri? You think I just might turn out to be, well, pretty?"

Kerri nodded. "I do. And not just pretty, but beautiful."

Jane glowed. A warm colour came to her cheeks and her eyes lit up with a tawny light that reminded Kerri of a stream running sparklingly over brown stones flecked with moss. It was only later when they heard a car roar up the driveway in front of the house that Kerri became ill at ease. They turned and saw Dominic stride into the house, carrying a briefcase under one arm.

Later he joined them and Kerri felt a

sudden shyness seize her as she endured his raking gaze and for a moment her self-assurance deserted her completely. However, apart from a brief, "Good morning" to the two girls he ignored them, seating himself on a canvas chair under a brightly striped umbrella farther along the beach and proceeding to read a sheaf of typescript.

He was still wearing his suit, although he removed the jacket after a few minutes and undid the knot in his tie.

Kerri swam a way out and let herself float in the tepid water, gazing towards the beach with its feathery green palm trees growing almost to the water's edge, and the glimpse of gayly flowering shrubs in the gardens behind.

Out to sea, beyond the coral reef, yachts with white sails glittered in the brilliant sunshine, and she wondered if they would get a chance to sail on one. It would be wonderful, in waters like these . . .

She heard a voice calling and with a start she looked towards the beach to see Dominic standing, one finger slotted in the pages of manuscript to mark his place. He called again. "Miss Matheson, I suggest you come in now, it's almost lunchtime."

The morning had flown so quickly that Kerri could hardly believe it. With a few fast strokes she reached the shore and bent to reach her towel, but Dominic was there before her. With a smile he held it out and as their fingers touched, for one brief instant Kerri felt such a shock that she almost dropped the towel. Avoiding his amused gaze, she wrapped the towel beneath her arms, sarong fashion, and went to call Jane who seemed to be deliberately ignoring her uncle's summons.

After lunch they went back to the beach, dropping down on their stomachs to sunbathe. From where she lay Kerri had a good view of Dominic. She noticed he was once more deep in the study of his work and she wondered what could be so almighty enthralling to take his attention away from the fantastic scenery and the warm Polynesian sunshine. She watched as the grim set of his features never relaxed for a moment, not realising that she in turn was being watched.

Jane coughed, rolled over on her back and raising herself on one elbow, murmured, "You like him, don't you?"

Kerri was thunderstruck. Shocked, she managed to exclaim, "Your uncle? You must be joking!"

"Then why do you work for him?"

Kerri shrugged. "He pays me a salary, but that doesn't mean I have to like him."

"But you do, I can always tell. Most women go mad over Dominic. But however much they try it never gets them anywhere. He doesn't like women, you see. Oh," hastily amending her comment, "some women, yes. They visit him at the house sometimes . . . "

She paused, looking at Kerri beneath tangled lashes, waiting for her to ask the usual questions. Women always did. They wondered why he wasn't married, why there was never a girlfriend in evidence.

If she thought Kerri was in the least bit curious, though, she was in for a disappointment. Kerri gathered a handful of sand, so fine it was almost like white sugar, and watched it as it trickled through her fingers. When she didn't speak, Jane went on, curiously, "Well, aren't you going to ask what kind of women visit him at the house sometimes?"

Kerri laughed and shook her head. "No. It doesn't really matter, does it? What your uncle does with his private life is his concern. I'm here for the summer merely to keep you company, and after that I don't suppose we'll ever see one another again, any of us."

Why, she wondered, did her heart give that silly little lurch at such a thought? After she had finished here, there would be no possible *reason* why she should ever meet Dominic Prentice again.

Looking thoughtful at Kerri's answer, Jane said musingly, "He's only thirty-seven, you know, not really old. I should think he'd be fantastic in bed . . . "

"Jane!" Embarrassed at the subject that had somehow sprung up between them, Kerri stood up, brushing the sand from her legs, and said, "I think I'll go and take another dip. It shouldn't be too soon after lunch now, should it?"

They left the beach as the sun set in a riot of colours over the ocean. There was no mistaking Dominic's imperious signal as he rose from his chair and, holding the file that contained his papers under one arm, he began to stride back to the house.

Once there they went their separate ways. On the threshold of his bedroom door, he turned to say, in his curt, managing way, "After dinner, I thought maybe a drive along the coast to Maili. What do you ladies think about that?"

Jane gasped and exclaimed, "Super!"

Her small flushed face lifted eagerly to her uncle. Kerri didn't answer, as, really, no reply seemed expected of her. She would have had to agree with his suggestion whatever she thought, wouldn't she, she reminded herself. And the outing did sound fun . . .

Jane made happy small talk all the way through dinner and snuggled next to her uncle in the front seat of the car as they began their drive afterwards. Kerri was forced to sit in the back alone, but she didn't really mind. Almost oblivious to the gay chatter of the girl, Jane, she gazed enthralled at the panoramic view offered in the bright moonlight.

She felt swallowed up in the luxury of the swiftly moving car. She felt she wanted to soak up as much of this wonderful atmosphere as she could before returning to the rather humdrum life of High Linton.

The two girls had dressed carefully for the occasion, Kerri in her one and only semi-evening gown, the white polyester, and Jane in the palest of pinks. She looked sweet and young and, Kerri could tell, was on her best behaviour. A far cry from the sulky, petulant girl of yesterday.

She saw the way Dominic looked at them, saw how he frowned when Jane, examining with critical eyes Kerri's white gown, said, "Don't you have anything else to wear, Kerri?"

Kerri flushed slightly, then her small chin lifted as she answered, "I'm afraid not. Why?" gazing down at the simple white dress. "What's wrong with this?"

Jane's nose wrinkled. "Nothing, I

suppose. It's just that it's so — plain. You need something to brighten it up. Necklaces. Lots of them, gaily coloured ones."

"Don't be personal, Jane." Her uncle's voice was clipped. "I think Miss Matheson looks very nice."

Kerri felt her cheeks flame at the amenity in his eyes. Something she had never expected to see there — for her . . .

She had to admit that he himself looked striking in his evening clothes and seemed less ill at ease, even managing to smile occasionally. She tore her gaze from the scenic beauty through which they were passing and watched the outline of his head, and his profile as he sat in front of her, and she wondered that the cold, proud face of Dominic Prentice should be so suddenly vivid in her mind. She gave a little shudder, thinking back to Jane's words about the women in her uncle's life, and the blatant, sexual attraction of the man that, no matter what one thought of him, one couldn't escape.

She was so immersed in her own thoughts that at first she did not notice the large white building that sparkled with lights before which they were pulling up. Dominic parked the car and with his usual perfunctory glance in their direction, led the way inside the building.

The Hotel Topaze was filled to overflowing and the sound from the small band was so gay and rhythmic she found herself longing to dance. But to her disappointment, and, she could see, Jane's too, they didn't stay long enough for that. Jane was so obviously in her seventh heaven that, from the gay animation of a moment ago, the small face took on a rebellious look when Dominic remarked, a short time later, it was time to go.

"Do we have to?" Jane pouted. "We've only just got here, Dominic."

"Yes, we have to," her uncle said. "I'm leaving for the mainland in the morning. The plane leaves before six, so I'm afraid tonight we must all be early birds again."

Jane made not the slightest effort to hide her displeasure. She leaned across the table, the brown eyes full of urgent appeal. "Oh, Dominic, no! We only got here yesterday and already you're leaving us."

Dominic Prentice looked impatient. "We haven't all come to Lessane to enjoy ourselves, Jane, much as we'd like to." His voice was implacable. "I am a busy man and I have my commitments."

Kerri looked down at her hands. She doubted if he even knew how to enjoy himself.

"I have an interview arranged with the director of the Polynesian Museum," he went on, "Miss Matheson will keep you company. I'll return just as soon as I've completed my business."

The glowering look on Jane's face relaxed a bit at his words. "Oh, all right, then. I suppose if you must, you must. After all, I should be used to being left on my own by now."

"You won't be on your own. You'll be with Miss Matheson."

Jane shrugged, avoiding Kerri's eye. "Big deal! I suppose you expect me to do handstands, thinking of that?"

Her uncle pushed his drink to one side and, leaning over the table, said with tight lips, "You will please remember, young lady, that Miss Matheson is here as your companion and will be treated with respect. I seem to recall going over all this before with you, but I don't appear to have made much impression. I saw no harm in giving you a taste of the rather limited nightlife of the island, but if we are going to experience this childish petulance each time we go anywhere, perhaps we would do better to stick to the house and our own stretch of beach."

He finished the sentence with a penetrating glance at Kerri. Again she lowered her gaze to her hands, thinking that if he ever had occasion to speak like that to her she would surely feel like sinking through the floor.

However, his rather caustic words didn't seem to bother Jane, for rising, she pranced haughtily ahead, her pale blonde hair swinging on her shoulders.

The drive back to the house was made in silence. Once there, Jane went straight to her room, without a backward glance, not even a murmured goodnight. Dominic Prentice stood, watching her go, then lowered his head to say to

Kerri, "She's spoiled, I'm afraid, and her manners are atrocious. The school was recommended most highly, but good manners seem to be low on its list of subjects."

Plainly embarrassed, Kerri replied, "It's probably her age. Growing up these days is no fun. In a year or two you won't know her."

Dominic's lips twitched. "What a hope to hang on to, Miss Matheson. Growing up in any age is no fun. Now," and his voice took on a businesslike tone, "as regards your duties for the next few days. I think by now you know what is required of you. I can but rely on you to see that no harm comes to Jane while I am away. It won't be easy, not in her present mood," and again his lips twitched, "but I've no doubt that you will overcome it."

He fixed her with such a piercing gaze that although her temper stirred at his speculative tone all she could do was murmur, in a small voice, "I understand."

"Excellent! Then I'll say goodnight."

They walked into the house together.

When he was to move away to go to his room Dominic turned and said, "I will, of course, complete my business as quickly as possible, but should you wish to contact me, the Polynesian Museum will know my whereabouts."

He looked at her as though he expected her to say something and when she merely nodded to signify she understood, he added, brusquely, "Of course, it would have to be important. Desperate, even. Otherwise . . . "

He left the sentence unfinished, but as she let herself into her room Kerri thought she knew perfectly well what he had been going to say.

"Otherwise don't bother me . . . "

Although she was sleepy, Kerri stood for a while by her open window. All kinds of misgivings had suddenly overtaken her now that her responsibility really had began. Now she was to have Jane solely under her control, she wondered if she would be capable of dealing with the rather spoiled and wayward girl.

Foolish of her, but she felt almost abandoned. She sighed, and looked out to where a line of white surf, just visible in the darkness, marked the edge of the water. The soft purring of a car engine made her lean out farther, resting her hands on the broad sill. Below her, clearly visible, a long sleek limousine came to a smooth halt and a woman got out. There was a shimmer of pale silk, moon shining on thick black hair and Kerri was just in time to see the tall figure of Dominic Prentice stride from the front door to meet her.

Kerri watched them embrace, the woman's bare arms lifting to pull the man's head down to her's. She saw their lips meet. It was a long, lingering kiss. Dominic was in his bathrobe, his feet and legs bare, and the towelling robe held loosely together revealed his brown chest almost to the waist.

"Dominic, *chéri!*" The husky, seductive voice came clearly to Kerri's ears. She did not hear Dominic's reply. She had shrunk away convulsively from the broad windowsill. For a moment she stood, then with a feeling of melancholy sweeping over her such as she had never experienced before, she went to bed.

6

MORNING came with the sound of birds and the sighing of the breeze in the palms. Gardeners spoke in soft voices, merging with the hum of a lawn-mower. It was as though some blessed genie had waved a wand and the island had suddenly sprung to life. Across the garden the sky was a tropical blue, with the ocean merging on the horizon into a misty, purple haze.

At this hour the beaches in both directions would be deserted and standing by her window, trying not to think about last night, a thin cotton négligé thrown about her, Kerri thought what a wonderful hour it would be for a quiet swim. She would have the water to herself. Already she was smitten by the island. She couldn't think why she had been so concerned last night at the little scene below her window.

Dominic Prentice was a virile man. As Jane had mentioned, there would be many women in his life. But, then, she had to admit that she also had been concerned about Dominic's news that he would be away for a while and she would have complete control of Jane. A job like this would bring worries, she couldn't expect it not to, not with a girl like Jane. But it was worth it. Where else could she expect to be paid to do absolutely nothing but enjoy herself and keep an eye on her charge while doing so?

Gazing at the azure sea, the ring of coral far out where waves beat high, bursting with white thunder over the protecting reef, she told herself nothing could be more agreeable. In spite of her aversion to her employer . . .

Kerri had to admit that she would have been happier if he had remained a totally unknown quantity to her — in fact, the less she saw of him the better. No man had ever spoken or looked at her the way he did, and she was only too aware how her pulses quickened and her mouth went oddly dry each time she caught his glance.

Uncomfortably aware, too, of those

muscular shoulders under the well-tailored suits and the assurance of those piercing eyes that suggested he was not a man to be trifled with. Heaven knew how he would react if she allowed anything to happen to Jane while he was away . . . Smiling to herself, she turned from the window to find her swimsuit and towel.

When she got to the beach she found that already the water was like tepid milk, and the air quickly turning hot and sultry. She put on her goggles and kicked down to the seabed, to a world of submarine Technicolor, perfectly clear to her through her huge goggles.

Everything seemed to move in slow motion; the colourful marine life that darted past, the barely moving plants that gave the impression of a huge underwater forest. Afterwards, sitting on the warm sand, arms clasped round her drawn-up knees, she sat and gazed at the perfect scene.

It was early yet, no hurry to wake Jane, who hated the act of rising from her bed, anyway, even in this wonderful place.

Kerri let her thoughts wander. Who

was the woman who had arrived last night, quietly and secretively, who had kissed so passionately below her window and who had accompanied Dominic into the house? Had the woman spent the night here, and, even if she had, why should that concern her, Kerri Matheson? Her remark to Jane came back to taunt her, "What your uncle does with his private life is his concern."

What if he had women friends with whom he slept! It was no affair of her's. Her job was to keep an eye on Jane, not her uncle . . .

She arrived back at the house in time to see a sleepy Jane emerging from her bedroom. Breakfast was already waiting on the terrace; deliciously cool slices of pawpaw sprinkled with lemon juice to start, with coffee and toast to finish. Jane seemed in a more cheerful frame of mind than last night and after breakfast suggested they get Morello, her uncle's handyman and chauffeur, to drive them into Maili, to do some shopping.

"I need some new clothes," she announced, grimacing down at the attractive yellow sundress she had put

90

on. "I've worn these old things so many times that I'm heartily sick of them."

'These old things!' thought Kerri, wryly, looked as though they had originally cost a packet, but she kept her silence. She had decided that the best way to get on , with the younger girl was to simply fall in with her wishes. As far as possible, anyway.

She agreed that a drive into town would be fun, and there was always shopping she could do herself. She would buy a picture postcard to send to her parents and Neil, informing them of her safe arrival, and that everything was far more wonderful than she had envisaged.

After breakfast they got a maid to ask Morello to bring the car to the front of the house. The drive into town, along a narrow, sun-dappled road lined with tall, leafy trees, was pleasant, with the car windows rolled down and the salt-laden breeze teasing their hair. This was the same road they had taken last night, Kerri realised, to the hotel, but in daylight it seemed vastly different.

Jane, it seemed, had more than an adequate allowance, and although Kerri couldn't hope to compete with her in the small amount of money she had with her, relying on her forthcoming salary, she managed to obtain the few things she required.

On the beach, they came across a young native boy selling lengths of brightly coloured cotton muslin. The colours were really vivid — oranges, lime greens, scarlets, royal blues . . .

He showed Kerri how to tie a length low on her hip, to wear the top of her bikini above and allow the loose ends of the scarf-like material to move with the sea breezes. She chose one in shell pink, with the scarlet of hibiscus blossom and pale green leaves printed on it. Jane purchased a length with a black background, on which a vivid pattern of yellow, blue and red flowers entwined with green leaves. Kerri could hardly persuade her that again it was hardly suitable for a young girl to wear, but she prayed that the girl would keep it to wear some time when her uncle was absent on one of his business calls.

In the bazaar Jane also bought a length of lime green silk which she said she would have made up by one of the Indian dressmakers who abounded on the island. Kerri fingered a length of silver shot with emerald green while the girl made her arrangements with the stall-holder who knew all the tailors and seemed to work in conjunction with them. Wistfully, Kerri said she wished she could afford the silver material but she was afraid her money wouldn't stretch that far.

Jane, who had just finished paying the man, was immediately contrite, and Kerri was astonished to hear her exclaim, "I'm sorry, I never thought. Won't you let me . . . ?"

Guessing what she was about to say, Kerri quickly shook her head. "No. Thanks, but really I can get it another time."

The younger girl looked at her, a sullen frown on her face. "Well, there's no need to be so snooty about it."

"I'm sorry, I didn't mean to sound snooty. It's just that I don't like borrowing."

Jane turned away, her face flushed, but to Kerri's relief she soon seemed to put the incident out of her mind. They pushed their way through the throng of people who crowded the bazaar. Most of them were dark-skinned. The men, tall and muscular, with frizzy hair, wore vividly coloured shirts and khaki shorts, the women were in simple dresses, although a number of the younger girls wore sarongs with hibiscus and frangipangi in their luxuriant dark hair.

Afterwards the girls sat under a striped umbrella at a beach-front café and sipped fresh chilled pineapple juice through straws. Kerri was glad to relax, watching the people as they sauntered past. No one, it seemed, hurried in this climate. Everyone seemed to be in the best of spirits, smiling, talking, completely inhibited in their attitude to one another.

After a while Kerri noticed with a sense of shock that the younger men were pausing as they came abreast of their table and that Jane was returning the open invitation in their dark eyes with smiles of her own. In fact, her whole demeanour was frighteningly adult.

Her laughter rang out, clear and tinkling. Her chatter became gay and animated and her eyes sparkled with open invitation. Fortunately, few of the local gallants understood or could speak English and after a while Kerri found she was more amused than anything else at Jane's behaviour. One young man, obviously an American, with sun-bleached hair and bronzed skin, towered above the rest of the crowd and more than once Kerri caught his eyes fixed on Jane.

The girl's sudden vivacity increased as she, too, became aware of his interest. The sun began its gradual descent, a miracle in Technicolor, and Morello appeared. He seemed a little concerned that the young ladies were staying so late and reminded them how swiftly darkness fell in this latitude.

They made their way back to the car, Morello carrying Jane's multitude of parcels, pushing ahead as they followed.

They were ravenous and after a shower and a change into fresh clothes, they sat on the terrace, sipping fruit juice and listening to a new long-playing record that Dominic had bought somewhere. It was one of the Mozart piano concertos, but after a while Jane asked her to switch it off, wrinkling her nose as the lovely piano notes, like drops of icy water, Kerri thought, refreshing and wholly delicious, filled the room. Jane said, as Kerri rose to lift the needle from the record, "I suppose it's all right for people like Dominic, he enjoys that sort of thing, but it's not my style at all."

People like Dominic! thought Kerri wryly. People like Dominic Prentice enjoyed all sorts of things this girl would never, in a hundred years, appreciate.

She said, trying to keep the sarcasm from her voice, "I suppose you'd prefer the Rolling Stones or something equally noisy."

She would never know why she said that, for not so long ago her own taste of music ran to groups like the one she had mentioned. Had this lovely island, with its quiet beaches and invigorating sunshine changed her all that much? Made her grow up far quicker than she would have done in High Linton? Above all, given her an appreciation of things Dominic Prentice liked?

What nonsense, she told herself. Who

cared what Dominic Prentice liked. She certainly didn't. She placed the record in its sleeve and put it back in the rack where she had found it, and joined Jane once again on the terrace, where they discussed the exciting buys they had made in the bazaar at Maili.

The only moment of dissonance had been over Jane's offer to lend money, and Kerri still couldn't understand why the younger girl should have taken her refusal so personally. Surprisingly, Jane found a way to bring it up again after dinner as she said, casually; "Are your family poor?"

Kerri flushed and felt her back stiffen. "If, by poor you mean I can't afford the sort of clothes you can or a holiday spent like this," gesturing with a slim hand at their surroundings, "then yes, I suppose you could say that."

Jane digested this in silence. She studied the fingernails of one hand, freshly tipped with frosted coral, and murmured, "Have you any sisters or brothers?"

"One brother. His name is Neil."

"How old is he?" Jane tried to give

the impression of being only mildly interested.

"Older than me by three years."

"Is he married?"

Kerri shook her head. Her answer was an emphatic, "No, not Neil. I've yet to see the girl who can snare him."

Jane made no comment on this and silence overcame them as they sat gazing out at the dark blue sea. The only sound was that made by the surf and the far-off hum of a passing car. Jane seemed to have retired behind that wall of silence that sometimes overcame her and after they had finished their meal with coffee served on the terrace went to bed.

The following afternoon they again took the car, this time back to the hotel, Jane saying they could have tea there and look around the gardens and the swimming-pool area. A gilt-lettered notice in the foyer announced there would be dancing that night. The band was a new one and a singer of some modest fame would be appearing.

"Super!" Jane's eyes shone. "Let's come. Morello can drive us here and bring us back afterwards."

Seeing the look on Kerri's face, she grimaced and said, scornfully, "Don't be such a drag! It could be fun."

Taken unawares, Kerri said, "It could also be dangerous. I don't think your uncle would approve."

"Dominic isn't here," Jane reminded her smoothly. "How is he going to know — unless," pursing her lips and looking at Kerri consideringly, "someone tells him."

Kerri had to admit that what the girl said was true. Besides, what harm could there be in a drive out in the cool of the evening, to sit and listen to music?

They spent some time getting ready and Kerri thought Jane looked pretty and very much more than her sixteen years in a dress of the palest lemon. She herself wore a full, short-skirted dress of peacock blue that wasn't really an evening dress but which would have to do.

She was too conscious of her responsibilities as chaperon to Jane to be truly looking forward to the evening, and half dreaded to think what Dominic would say if he found out. Hastily she amended that to *when* he found out.

The other way sounded too clandestine to be comfortable. And there was every possibility that he would. Some one on the staff would gossip. Possibly even Morello himself.

Still, she couldn't see what harm there could be in her and Jane sitting listening to the young singer. They would stay only an hour, at the most two, and be in bed long before midnight.

Morello, tight-lipped but prudently keeping his thoughts to himself, parked before the long flight of steps that led up to the hotel entrance. Slipping from behind the driving-wheel, he went round to open the door for the two girls to alight. Then, frowning, he drove the car to a side parking to await their return.

Jane, very much the young lady and completely at ease, sailed into the large room where the band was playing. They chose a table near the band and seated themselves. Kerri still feeling distinctly ill at ease. Jane's face glowed with excitement and her foot began to tap in time with the music. Within minutes she had a partner and although Kerri frowned and shook her head, not liking the look of the young man with frizzy hair who asked her so casually, Jane ignored her.

The youth was the first of many partners with whom Jane danced that evening. Kerri refused to dance time and again, thinking she really couldn't keep an eye on Jane and enjoy herself at the same time. She sat back, the smile stiff on her lips, and told herself she was being over-sensitive. After all, what possible harm was there in Jane enjoying herself in this way?

So she sipped her orange juice and tried to relax, hoping that Dominic Prentice would see it in the same light. The evening passed and to Kerri's surprise Jane made no objections when she glanced pointedly down at her tiny wrist-watch and said wasn't it time they were going. Jane collected her small silver evening bag and, rising calmly, preceded her to the foyer.

Feeling more like a formidable matron aunt than anything else, Kerri waited beside the other girl at the top of the steps for Morello to bring the car round, smiling in spite of herself at the injured looks Jane's admirers directed at her. 'Sorry, guys,' she thought, ruefully, 'come back in about two years' time.'

The house was all in darkness when they arrived back, and to Kerri's horror, she saw Dominic's Mercedes parked to one side of the driveway. Resolutely, she pushed the dreamy Jane in before her, closing the front door as silently as she could. She whispered a soft, "Goodnight," then closed Jane's bedroom door to tiptoe to her own room.

Feeling a rush of relief, she had turned the door handle and was pushing the door open when a voice, quiet and deceptively calm, from the shadows in the passage behind her, said, "Good evening, Miss Matheson. Or should I say good morning?"

Luckily for her, the shadows were deep and he didn't see the tell-tale flush of guilt that flooded her cheeks. "I — I know it's late," she began, and her voice took on a kind of desperation, although she told herself she was a fool to feel so guilty about something that was, after all, perfectly natural and innocent — a young girl enjoying herself in the company of other young people — "but the evening went so quickly and Jane was so enjoying herself, it seemed a shame to . . . "

"Drag her away?" he finished for her when she paused, seeing the cold disapproval in his eyes.

"It wasn't a bit like you think," she blurted out, angered at his look.

"Really!" The dark brows were raised questioningly. "And may I presume to know what you imagine I am thinking?"

Under his stringent gaze, she said, "By the way you are looking at me right now, I can imagine all sorts of things are going through your mind," adding wryly to herself, "and not one of them to my credit."

As though he followed the workings of her mind, he rapped, "Don't let's be provoking, shall we, Miss Matheson?"

Kerri winced at his expression. She looked down at her hand, still holding the doorknob. Although it meant biting her tongue, she would treat the whole matter calmly, matter-of-factly. How *could* he expect a girl as vivacious as his niece to shun the company of other young people, especially in this exotic sun-filled island and whilst on holiday. Surely he must know Jane better than that. Or did he suspect that Kerri was a willing partner in their search for an exciting nightlife?

Looking up she saw his face was wooden, and a small muscle flexed in his jaw as he said, icily, "It might be better if we discussed this matter in more detail tomorrow. I'll see you in my study after breakfast."

He gave her a long, steely look, then added, "Goodnight, Miss Matheson."

Feeling like a Victorian scullery-maid dismissed by the squire, completely shattered by the events of the last few minutes, Kerri wasted no time in getting undressed and between the sheets.

The next morning the sun shone down in happy ignorance of the intimidating events of the night before. They breakfasted as usual on the terrace and to Kerri's vast relief Dominic didn't appear.

During the meal Jane blurted out that her uncle had arrived back unexpectedly. She thought he might have come out to bid them good morning, although he didn't often eat breakfast.

Kerri wondered if he had already tackled his niece about their activities of the night before. Then she knew he had when Jane made the remark that her uncle was "in a bit of a mood", adding, ruefully, "I'm sure if he and my father had their way, they would keep me safely hidden away at school for the whole year."

Feeling decidedly nervous at the thought of the forthcoming interview, Kerri could barely manage a smile. Jane, with a reasoning that surprised Kerri, remarked, "I *thought* I heard voices in the passage last night. I take it the vibrations between you and my uncle are not very harmonious at the moment."

Kerri wrinkled her nose. "You take it right. In fact, the vibrations are distinctly turbulent. Your uncle wants to see me in his study after breakfast."

"Gee, Kerri!" Jane looked dismayed. "I'd better come with you. Dominic's quite formidable when he gets going and you'll need all the backing you can get."

Kerri took a deep breath and leaned forward in her chair to pour herself more coffee. The breeze from the ocean lifted her hair from her face, showing the tell-tale flush that deepened at the girl's words.

"I'm sure I can handle it, Jane, but if I can't . . . " She broke off, seeing again the hard menacing eyes that had gazed at her so chillingly last night in the shadowy passage. The streamlined silver coffee-pot shook slightly in her hand, spilling some of the dark liquid into her saucer.

"Hey!" Jane's eyes opened wide. "You really *are* in a state! I really think I should go in with you and admit that it was all my idea."

At that moment one of the maids appeared in the open glass doors behind them. She asked softly if she could bring more toast and Kerri accepted eagerly. Anything to protract the time between now and the moment when she would have to face those cool, disapproving eyes again. She was dismayed at the way the thought made her tremble.

7

TEN minutes later, feeling weak and distinctly inept, she found herself standing in front of a heavily carved blackwood desk. Dominic's dark head was bent over a pile of typed papers spread out on the desk before him, and damn him! she thought, he's doing it on purpose — he made her wait for a few moments while he leisurely corrected a sentence or two.

At last he lifted his head and, well-manicured hands resting flat on the desktop, he looked up at her. A slight smile touched the corners of his mouth.

"Good morning. Do please be seated, Miss Matheson. You really mustn't look at me like that, you know. I'm not going to eat you."

Her cheeks flushed scarlet but she did as she was bid, sitting straight and still, stiff with pride.

He leaned back in his chair and made himself comfortable before beginning.

"Perhaps we could start with an explanation. Morello tells me he took you and my niece to the Hotel Topaze and although he distinctly got the impression the whole thing was Jane's idea, he seemed to think you gladly went along with it." His eyes fixed her steadily and it took all her self-control to keep from squirming under that cold gaze.

She blurted out, feebly, "Jane was very insistent. I did try to stop her, pointing out that you might not like it, but she wouldn't listen and, really, Mr Prentice," feeling her nerve coming back, "I saw no harm in listening to the music of the band and the singer *is* quite well known . . ."

He sliced off her rambling with, "I understood that you were fully aware of just *how* insistent, as you put it, my niece can be. If you aren't, Miss Matheson, then perhaps I'd better try to explain once more exactly what your duties are. The nightclub belonging to the Topaze has a reputation that I do not like. Certainly do not want my niece to become mixed up with."

"But you yourself took us there in

the first place!" Kerri's voice held indignation.

He looked at her witheringly. "That was entirely different. *I* was with you. Two young women alone — well, that's a very different matter."

The door behind them suddenly swung open and Jane came in, walking stiffly. She stopped beside Kerri and faced her uncle across the desk. "Please, Dominic, don't blame Kerri like that. It was mostly my fault."

She caught her breath on the sentence, gazing at him as his face darkened. "Am I to understand, that besides deliberately disobeying my orders, you also listen to private conversations outside doors?" he rasped.

"Oh, Dominic!" Jane's voice rose in a wail. "We were only having some fun. You," and the innuendo in her voice made Kerri start nervously, "you aren't above inviting — friends, to stay the night . . . "

Before Kerri's eyes there flashed a scene — a smoothly purring car below her window, the tall, slim figure of a woman stepping out, to be greeted by Dominic Prentice. Greeted very affectionately, too . . .

Dominic drew a deep breath and hunched forward in his chair. "Now, you listen to me, young lady. Any more of this kind of behaviour and you'll find yourself back with Miss Boguy at school, so fast that you won't know what hit you. Do you understand?"

"Yes, Dominic," came the meek reply, although Kerri caught a hint of defiance still in the low voice.

"I don't have to explain myself to you," Dominic went on, bitingly. "But Miss Dalny is an old and valued friend and as she happened to be flying to the mainland I invited her to share the plane I had chartered."

"Yes, Dominic," came the quiet answer.

"So from now on I don't want to hear another word about gallivanting out at night, unless I am here to accompany you. Is that clear?" And although he spoke to Jane his gaze swung to Kerri.

"Yes, Dominic," murmured Jane for the third time.

He pursed his lips and leaned back in his chair, studying them both. Dismayed that their thoughtless — and perhaps foolish — action had resulted in all this, Kerri said, softly, "I really am sorry, Mr Prentice. Truly. I didn't think you would mind Jane having fun with people her own age . . . She wasn't out of my sight for one minute . . . "

"What about when *you* were dancing, Miss Matheson?" His voice was grave although she saw the teasing smile that wrinkled the corners of his eyes.

Before she could answer, Jane said, "Kerri didn't dance. Not at all. She sat like a maiden aunt watching me the entire evening."

Dominic let a long pause elapse and the irony now was very evident, as he murmured, "How very commendable of Miss Matheson."

"There were plenty of guys who asked her," Jane went on, smiling reminiscently, "but she refused every time."

He gave his niece an amused look and said, "I'm glad to hear that she was at least cognizant with her duties. Now that that is cleared up to our satisfaction, if you don't mind, young lady, Miss

111

Matheson and I were having a private conversation."

He allowed the sentence to trail off, fixing Jane with a grave look.

The girl nodded understandingly and with a tight smile at Kerri she left the room, closing the door with exaggerated solicitude behind her. Kerri sat where she was, hoping to be dismissed, wondering at the same time what more he had to say to her.

Dominic rose to his impressive height and, coming round the desk, held out a small packet wrapped in tissue paper he had taken from the top drawer in the desk. As her slim fingers closed about it, a puzzled look on her face, he said, "I hope you like coral. It's the prettiest I could find."

Stunned, she slowly slipped the ribbon off the tiny parcel and a moment later there fell into the palm of her hand a coral necklace of the most gorgeous shade of pink. She gasped with pleasure and looked up to meet his eyes. "It's — it's lovely . . . But why . . . ?"

Her puzzled frown said the rest and he smiled. "To wear with your white dress.

We can't have Jane making disparaging remarks each time you wear it, can we? I happened to see it in the window of a small jeweller's and thought you might like it. As I said, I hope you like coral."

"I love it. Thank you." Sensing that to express her thanks too emotionally would only embarrass him, she left it at that, bending her head over the string of beads in her lap. The silence seemed to stretch to eternity and at last, unable to deny the almost irresistible impulse, she raised her head to find, disconcertingly, that he was watching her.

Her colour rose and the trite remark she had been planning on — something about how envious her friends at home would be when they saw the beautiful and unique necklace — died on her lips.

Wonderingly, her eyes searched his face, marking the thick, dark eyebrows above those impenetrable grey eyes, the hard lines of his mouth and jaw. In spite of the casual beige slacks and the open-neck silk shirt he wore, she was aware of the strength of chest and shoulders they concealed, and the air of restless, barely controlled energy that so typified the man.

"Thank you again," she murmured, floundering a little under his gaze.

He drew deeply on the cigarette he was smoking. "My pleasure, Miss Matheson. Now, if you will excuse me . . . ?"

She nodded, rose and left the room. The rest of the morning was spent demurely, Jane writing letters to her friends from school and, Kerri thought, by the secret little smile that touched her mouth at intervals, romanticisms at lengths about the island.

Kerri read a novel she had brought with her, although every so often she had to bring her thoughts under control when they would insist on conjuring up the grey eyes and thick, black hair of her employer. She shivered in spite of herself as the dark, relentless features kept forcing themselves on her mind. She wondered at the anger he'd shown over her escapade with Jane at the Topaze, and later his kindness in buying her the coral necklace. Dominic Prentice! Her mouth turned down at the corners.

What a contrary man!

She gave a little trembling sigh. All she could hope for was to keep out of his way as much as possible and make sure Jane never again got the better of her. After all, he *was* paying her a salary, and a very fair one, to see that his niece behaved herself. Time would soon pass and the summer would be over and then there was no reason why she should ever have to set eyes on him again.

She woke early the next morning after a restless night. She showered and dressed in a pair of white, very brief shorts, showing the long, slim tan of her legs to advantage. She pulled on a yellow T-shirt over her head, tied her hair back with a white chiffon scarf, so that it hung low on her neck, then slipped out and let herself quietly into the kitchen.

The staff were already up and coffee was bubbling on the huge white stove. The cook, a huge, genial Polynesian woman who couldn't speak a word of English but who none the less seemed to understand Kerri's meaning, smiled widely and poured her a cup.

Carrying the cup, she went outside

to the terrace and sat with her face upturned to the sun, breathing in the heady perfume of the ginger blossom that grew in huge clumps on the edge of the lawn, the spade-like leaves topped with the creamy-white blossom that smelled so heavenly.

Presently she was joined by Jane and, to Kerri's surprise, her uncle, who announced casually that he would have to hurry as there was a boat leaving in an hour for the island of Kejo and he was sailing on it.

Jane pouted. "You're not leaving us again!" she said, accusingly. "Can't we come with you, Dominic?"

His gaze, brooding and enigmatic, rested briefly on her but it seemed to Kerri he was speaking to her when he replied, "To be honest, I never gave it a thought. Do you really think you'd enjoy visiting the hot springs and seeing men walk on hot stones? It's a ceremony I want to investigate more fully as a chapter of my book will describe it in detail."

Jane wrinkled her nose. "It might be better than hanging round here. Let's face it, *anything* is better than hanging around here. Especially when you are forbidden to go out and enjoy yourself."

Thankfully, her uncle chose to ignore her remark, much to Kerri's relief. Instead, he glanced down at his wrist-watch and said, "Well, if you'd like to come with me, then I suggest we all get a move on. The boat leaves at ten so we haven't much time."

Jane, in spite of her earlier enthusiasm, resumed her bored expression when she saw the old schooner they were to sail in. Battered by the weather, its once sparkling white paint blistered by the tropical sun, it looked awfully vulnerable, especially when one considered the razor-sharp coral reef through which they would have to pass, using a very narrow channel, and the huge waves that battered against it. Still, Kerri reassured herself, it must be safe, otherwise Dominic would never have suggested it.

The captain, an elderly Scotsman, seemed to be a friend of Dominic's and greeted the girls with open-armed enthusiasm. "Your niece, eh? And a friend! Lovely, lovely. Ye're welcome to the old *Sea Swallow*, m'dears. Prettiest

117

cargo we've had in a long while."

Below her breath, Kerri heard the other girl mutter, "Silly old duffer! Surely Dominic can do better than this!" and once again Kerri wondered at the changeable attitude of the girl. Kerri herself couldn't help but be thrilled at anything and everything that happened on this fascinating island.

It was unfortunate that Jane didn't feel the same. As the morning wore on, the girl became more and more morose and difficult to talk to. She ignored Kerri's exclamation of delight as they sailed into the blue inlet where beaches were strung like pearls along the coastline with palms growing to the water's edge. It was a place of light and shade, of beauty and quiet serenity. Darkly blue in deep water, almond green in the shallows, it lay redolent in the hot sun with the scent of drying vegetation wafting to them on the breeze, mingled with the inevitable fragrance of ginger.

Kerri stood back from the rail, watching as Dominic, followed by his niece, scrambled down the swaying rope-ladder to the small boat waiting below. Dominic had explained that the depth of the water was too shallow to allow the *Sea Swallow* to approach closer, so they would have to be rowed ashore in the dinghy.

Well, that was all right with her, Kerri thought. She was enjoying every moment of this wonderful day. Climbing down the gently swaying ladder, with Jane and Dominic already settled in the stern of the boat, Kerri let her gaze for a moment wander over the shimmering water below. From this height she could see the bottom, the fine white sand, the vividly coloured marine life that was everywhere.

Could any place be more beautiful? Surely not! Not in this whole wide world . . .

Immersed in her thoughts, her attention wandering, suddenly she felt her foot slipping and clutched desperately at the rope. It slipped through her fingers, burning her palms, and the next moment with a small scream she'd landed in the dinghy. Her fall caused it to rock violently and Jane cried out. Although Kerri was too shaken to hear what she said, she made a wild guess that it wasn't complimentary. The next moment arms went round her and she was lifted and held close in their strong clasp.

Close to her ear, Dominic's deep voice murmured, "Now that was a silly thing to do! Suppose I hadn't been here to catch you?"

"But you were." She gave a little smile and pushed him away. For a moment, a very brief moment, it seemed to Kerri that his arms tightened their grip and his eyes darkened. Then with a small laugh he let her go and she slipped away to perch herself next to Jane on the wooden seat.

Luckily for her he seemed in an extraordinarily good mood and didn't refer to her little accident again, although she felt a perfect idiot for being so clumsy. Once on the island he pointed out the small village, the only human habitation on the place, and the line of canoes drawn up before it on the sloping beach.

Then, telling the two girls to follow closely behind him, he took a narrow track that led through the almost impenetrable jungle towards the interior of the island. Around them as they walked the bird chorus was shrill, together with rustlings made, Kerri suspected, by small animals. At least, she thought, gazing nervously about her, she *hoped* they were small animals.

The track emerged into a wide clearing where grass huts stood in a semi-circle. The people of the island were tall and dark, good-looking in a majestic kind of way. The girls were dressed, as their contemporaries had been that time in the bazaar, in brightly coloured sarongs with scarlet hibiscus in their hair. The men were in a regalia that made the two girls gasp.

The long tail-feathers of some exotic bird together with the soft brown fur of small animals combined to make their head-dress, circling their frizzy hair like a halo. Necklaces made of sharks' teeth and beaten silver hung to their navels, while bangles of flattened silver were clasped tightly about their sinewy forearms. The lower part of their faces were daubed with white in various designs.

Their skirts, resembling vaguely the type worn in ancient times by Roman soldiers, wide strips of soft leather or some kind of bark, hung from their waist to just above their knees. They stood in a group, waiting for the throng of tourists, of which there were quite a few, others having arrived by a specially chartered launch, to sort themselves out.

The rest of the tribe, mostly older people with white hair, tended the fires. Kerri gazed with some trepidation at the large, smooth stones, sizzling and crackling with heat, from which the elders were shovelling away the red-hot stones. Dominic, standing a little apart from her and Jane, had his notebook out and was speaking to one of the elders. Kerri saw him smile, raise one hand in a kind of salute, and stride over to join them.

Jane determined, or so it seemed to Kerri, to endure the whole thing with as little grace as possible, said sulkily, "For heaven's sake, Dominic, what are we hanging round here for? How much longer before they start?"

He fixed her with an accusing eye. "Now don't give me that, young lady. I told you I didn't think you would enjoy it but you still insisted on coming. Now that you are here, you could at least *try* and look pleasant."

Before the girl could reply there was a terrific thudding of drums, and four men, each carrying a long narrow drum made from rawhide, appeared. Their hands moved so swiftly that Kerri could hardly follow their movements. The thudding increased to a crescendo and Kerri felt excitement mount inside her, felt her senses stirring with the sounds.

Slowly, hand in hand, the warriors began to walk over the red-hot stones, just as, Dominic explained, as Kerri's horrified gasp caught his attention, their forebears had done thousands of years before. "Their faith is so strong," he told the wide-eyed girls, "that they feel no pain."

Kerri found after a few minutes that she couldn't bear to look any more and turned away, shuddering. Their faith may be strong, she thought, but suppose, just for a moment, that faith wavered . . .

After her first gasp of horror, Jane, too, had turned away. "Ugh!" She looked at Kerri, grimacing. "And I thought this was going to be a fun day!"

"Your uncle *did* warn you," Kerri reminded her.

"I know. I just never imagined . . . " She gazed around them, at the avidly curious group of tourists, the barbarically costumed warriors and shuddered again. "I hate anything like this," she finished. "I'm always terrified that something will go wrong, that someone will get hurt."

Kerri smiled at her in sympathy. "I know. I feel exactly the same."

"Why stay, then, if you dislike it so much?"

Kerri shrugged. "We have to stay with your uncle, Jane. We can hardly start back to the boat on our own. Besides," glancing towards the low wooden tables that had been set up under the trees, and where young native girls were busy with hollowed-out gourds, "isn't there some kind of feast afterwards?"

"If there is, I can't say I'm all that crazy to stay for it," Jane exclaimed and turned away.

The thudding of the drums became less frantic, quietened, sinking into a soft, rhythmic pulse and in spite of herself Kerri's attention was captured.

She held her breath until she saw that the fire-walkers were all safely through their ordeal and now it was the girls' turn to entertain.

They swayed into the centre of the clearing, dressed in traditional grass skirts with flower garlands about their necks, slim hips jerking rhythmically to the measured beat. Fascinated, Kerri found herself standing close to Dominic, her entire being captivated by the lovely, dusky-skinned maidens.

"Fine way to keep slim," she heard Dominic whisper, bending his head towards her. "It seems incredible that they can become so solid in later life."

Kerri smiled, thinking of the plumply comfortable cook who was always so genial about Kerri's early morning cup of coffee, and the other matronly figures in their huge, all-enveloping cotton dresses, who stood proudly watching the young dancers. "Doesn't it?" she agreed, lifting her head to gaze up at him.

The light in the clearing was greeny-gold, the fierce rays of the sun muted by the tall trees. Dust motes floated in that gold atmosphere and Kerri wasn't to know how the percolating sunlight caught in her hair, turning the wispy curls that had escaped from the chiffon scarf to burnished copper.

Dominic felt something within him stir, something he'd long since thought dead, coming to life briefly during his insouciant interludes with other women, but, as he'd thought, extinguished for ever after the beautiful, faithless Emma . . .

His gaze took in the soft skin, flushed by the humidity of the clearing, the tiny beads of moisture on the short upper lip, and, eyes moving downward, the slightly parted lips, full, made for a man's kisses . . .

He jerked his mind back to the reality of his surroundings. You're letting the place get to you, old boy, he told himself regretfully.

The look in his eyes, swiftly, but not swiftly enough, hidden, was not lost on Kerri. There was such sensual reminiscence in that look that her very bones seemed to turn to water. A tight knot, half excitement, half fear, impeded her breathing. She wasn't sure what happened then, but suddenly the drums were silent, the dancers dispersing and herself being led across the clearing to the long tables covered in fresh green coconut fronds. She felt his fingers, firm and cool, against the bare skin of her upper arm, heard his voice as he handed her a beaker of amber gold liquid.

"*Maca!*" He smiled down into her eyes with only a trace of the mockery she was used to. "That means," he explained, "cheers, bottoms up, or what have you. Go on, drink up, it's very thirst-quenching."

Doubtfully, Kerri lifted the beaker to her nose and sniffed. "What is it?"

He laughed. "It's a drink made from the root of the pepper plant. I know it sounds awful, but you'll see, you'll enjoy it. It's so smooth you won't even taste it. Your body will feel like it's floating."

Kerri gave a half-smile. She wasn't sure that she wanted to feel as though her body was floating. Too many disturbing things were happening in that jungle clearing — sensations, emotions she hadn't known she was capable of. One didn't intentionally walk into danger. Not if one was wise . . .

8

FEELING at a loss, aware of those intent grey eyes on her, she took a gulp of the liquid. He laughed again. "Hey, steady on, you're supposed to sip it. I said you would feel as if your body was floating, not rocketing to the moon."

Her own laugh was shaky and she was suddenly alarmed to see that they were alone in the clearing, the rest of the tourists having wandered away. She decided she didn't really like the taste of the native drink, suspecting it was too potent by far for her unsophisticated taste, and after the first mouthful didn't touch it again.

Still, he had been kind enough to see that she had some refreshment and, turning to him, she said, "Thank you for getting me some. It was thoughtful of you. But," glancing about them, "you don't have to stay with me if you don't want to. Don't you have something else to do? Take notes for your book or something?"

"You must stop being so self-reproachful. I don't care for this new humility. It's quite out of character, Kerri my love."

Stung, she gave him a sudden glare, searching vainly for a retort that would give her satisfaction and he the grace to look confused, and was nonplussed to see that the old mockery had replaced the sombre look in his eyes.

"That's better," he said impassively. He put out a hand to take the beaker from her and his cool fingers lingered on the soft flesh of her arm.

Dry-throated, she said, "I think I'd better look for Jane . . . "

"Must you?" His hand slid up her arm, to the bare shoulder. It moved there in the lightest caress. The drums had started again, sinking to the merest murmur, making her think of heartbeats in that deserted clearing, and she was suddenly aware of just *how* alone they were, and was tremblingly conscious of her own vulnerability. Her eyes, in the dimness of the clearing, gazed up at him, a deep velvety purple.

"Just listen to those drumbeats!" His voice was a whisper. "Don't they do things to your soul?"

She watched his face as he bent his head towards her and thought with some kind of dreamy wonder that she should move, slip away from this calm, yet dangerous place, while there was still time, join the other tourists who were probably buying souvenirs in the tiny gift shop on the beach.

But she did none of those things. She waited until his lips brushed her's, the merest caress, slow, almost teasing, a kiss that promised yet held at bay at the same time, until at last with a little protesting murmur, she pushed his hands convulsively away. "No, don't, I don't want you to . . . I ought to be looking for Jane, she's been gone rather a long time . . . "

His grin was lopsided as he gazed down at her. "You can't gaze at a man like that, with those huge, pansy eyes, and not expect him to do something about it." For a long moment he stood looking down at her, and then when he felt the shudder that went through her, he released her. "I'm sorry," he murmured. "I apologise. I didn't mean to offend you. Put it down to the music, or," with a grimace, "the drink."

When she didn't answer, he straightened, flexing his shoulders under the denim shirt he wore. "All right, go and find Jane if you're so worried about her. No doubt after that — degrading episode, you must be impatient to return to the boat and the rest of the group."

He turned abruptly and left her. She waited until he was out of sight, then sunk to the grass, her knees shaking under her. In just a few moments her entire feelings for Dominic Prentice had changed, she thought in bewilderment. She pressed the palm of one hand to her mouth, feeling again that kiss. She had felt completely helpless against his strength, helpless to deny the sweet flood of response his kiss aroused.

In spite of herself, little tongues of flames had flickered along her nerve ends in a devastating siege to her will. It was one of the white-haired elders coming back to the clearing that finally aroused her. She went in search of Jane. She found her to one side of the clearing, talking in animated fashion to a tall blond youth. Jane's cheeks flushed with annoyance when Kerri explained she thought her uncle wanted to be going. "Oh, all right, Kerri."

She turned back to the blond boy and said, scathingly, "My master's voice! See ya."

The trip back was uneventful. Jane stood next to Kerri at the rail, watching the island recede into the dim blue distance and the villagers wave them farewell from the white sand. The girl's recent vivaciousness seemed to have elapsed with the disappearance of the blond young man and Kerri wondered who he was. She saw the slim lines of a yacht with its white sails billowing in the wind anchored just beyond where their own boat had docked, all ready for sailing. She thought the boy had probably come in that. Perhaps one of the crew.

He had seemed rather nice. Good-looking in a boyish sort of way. In a year or two Jane would no doubt fall in love with a boy like that.

Kerri turned, her back to the rail and the sparkling topaz sea, and her eyes searched the deck for Dominic. She saw him standing a little way along from them, talking to the Scots captain. They seemed to be the best of friends and she thought she'd never seen Dominic so cordial, laughing loudly at the old captain's reminiscences. Her eyes lingered on Dominic's face, on the magnificent body in its denim jeans and open-necked denim shirt. The tight trousers accentuated the muscular length of his legs and he wore rope-soled sandals with canvas tops. The emotions she had felt in the clearing, felt again now with the memory so fresh in her mind, must have shown on her face, for beside her she heard Jane say, softly, almost scornfully, "My uncle has a disturbing effect on you, doesn't he, Kerri? I find it strange that he hasn't noticed it himself before now."

"Really, Jane." Kerri turned to face her, voice level. "I don't know where you get the idea that I like him, but you're under a misapprehension, you know. I have absolutely no interest in

133

your uncle other than he happens to be my employer, and pays my salary. In fact, although I shouldn't say it, and I trust," the soft mouth quirking, "that you won't repeat what I say, but there are times when I find him almost objectionable."

She turned back to the rail, leaning her forearms on the sun-warmed top, her heart hammering in spite of her words of scorn.

"So!" Jane gave a soft, mocking whistle. "The little scene I witnessed in the clearing after he'd offered you that bowl of repulsive drink didn't mean a thing, then?" She sighed, making a theatrical thing of it. "I was beginning to hope that dear Uncle Dominic had at last found someone he could share his life with, or at least become so preoccupied with romance that he would have less time to worry about me."

Her smile mocked the older girl and Kerri found herself flushing, "Shame, so I misread the situation completely. I ask your pardon, Kerri."

"So you should," Kerri answered her reprovingly. "You had no right to be spying on us in the first place, and in the second place, perhaps I'm over-sensitive on the subject, Jane, but I'm getting a bit tired of you assuming I'm some kind of silly — teenager, who has fallen madly in love with your uncle."

Jane's mobile mouth quirked. "Well, haven't you? Most other women he comes in contact do."

She gazed at Kerri with enigmatic brown eyes and Kerri for a moment hovered between annoyance and laughter. Then laughter won. "Well, I can assure you that I am not one of those women. In fact, the opposite might be more in keeping with my feelings for your uncle." She drew a deep breath of the salt-laden air. "Anyway, I'm surprised that the situation interests you so much, Jane. Personally, I find the whole subject pretty tedious. Why don't we talk about something else? For instance," smiling into the flushed face, "who was the boy *you* were talking to? He looked nice."

"Nice!" Jane wrinkled her nose in disgust. "What a description for Mark. He's fabulous."

"Is that his name?" Kerri gazed thoughtfully at the younger girl, wondering if she should treat it so lightly or if Dominic should be informed. "How did you happen to meet him?"

"Questions! Questions!" Jane exclaimed protestingly, and turned away so that Kerri couldn't see her face. "Can't I do *any*thing without being questioned like a six-year old?"

Kerri gave a sympathetic chuckle. "I'm sorry, love. From the glimpse I got of you both I sort of had the impression that you'd met previously. I mean, before today."

Jane gave her a mutinous glare. "Then you would be wrong, wouldn't you? Besides, when do I ever get the chance to meet *any*one, here in this God-forsaken place, with you as my custodian?"

After that there was little time to discuss further Jane's feelings or anything else, for just at that moment there were shouts and whistles from the native crew and the short gang-plank rattled on to the moss-covered quay.

Kerri turned to seek out Dominic, just in time to see the tall figure of the man step on to the wooden gangplank, and at the same moment there was a shriek from the small crowd of people waiting on the quay and she saw the slim figure of the woman run up to meet him. The same woman she had seen that night going into the house with Dominic's arm around her waist.

And then he was gazing up to where she and Jane waited at the rail, on Jane's face that knowing smile that irritated Kerri so much — 'So,' she thought, 'she has proved her point. Dominic Prentice *is* irresistible to most women. Only,' soft mouth poised she took a deep breath, 'I wouldn't be such a weak fool as to be one of his conquests.'

Beside her she heard Jane whisper, "That's Mrs Dalny. Nicole Dalny. She's one of Dominic's . . ." She let the sentence trail away, gazing at Kerri in that infuriatingly knowing way. Kerri chose not to answer and, after what seemed like an eternity but was in reality only a few minutes, she heard his voice calling to them, "Jane! Kerri! Come *on*. I don't feel like being all day."

No, thought Kerri, sarcastically, you certainly don't! Not with that — that female waiting eagerly for your embraces.

137

The woman had her own car waiting and Dominic chose to go with her, leaving Jane and Kerri to return to the house with Morello. In the car, Jane said, a certain amount of smugness in her voice, "You see what I meant when I said that about Dominic?"

Without speaking, Kerri nodded, her gaze intent on the passing scenery, not wanting the girl to see how much the recent little scene, with the memory of Dominic's kiss still warm on her lips, had disturbed her. She shrank away from the thought and it took almost all the physical effort at her command to turn to Jane and answer, calmly, "Yes, I see what you mean."

She lay awake for a long time that night, thinking of Dominic, thinking of Nicole Dalny and what she was to Dominic, wondering how much of the scene in the clearing Jane had witnessed — had she been watching when Dominic kissed her? — above all, remembering Dominic's hand on her shoulder, his lips on her's . . .

Finally, too restless to settle, she pushed the bedclothes back and slipped her feet to the floor. She padded to the dressing-table to open the small top drawer to lift out the coral necklace Dominic had given her. For a long time she stood holding it to her, in the palm of her hand, then with a sigh she replaced it in the drawer and went to the window.

Outside all was darkness. A deep silence hung over the island; tonight even the sound of the surf seemed strangely distant.

Sighing, she went back to her bed and drew on the silk kimono that lay across the foot, one of her purchases that morning with Jane at the bazaar, and drew the silk tie belt tightly about her slim waist. Then, walking on tiptoe, she opened her door and went along the passage to the large empty lounge.

She looked around, the light from the moon shining in the huge glass doors giving her just enough light to see by, and after a brief hesitation she went over to the settee across the back of which lay Dominic's jacket. One he had removed and thrown carelessly on to the settee just before they had left on the boat trip, saying it was too warm a day for a jacket.

She picked it up and bending her head held her cheek to the rough tweedy material, the spicy after-shave lotion he used, plus the pungent aroma of tobacco so evocative of the man.

She was just straightening when she suddenly knew beyond any doubt that she was no longer alone in the room.

She whirled around, her hand flying to her mouth as she saw the dark shadow watching her.

"Looking for something, Kerri?" inquired Dominic's cool voice from the doorway.

He came into the room, his feet soundless on the soft carpet and closed the door behind him. "What on earth are you doing here at this hour?" His voice was still polite but the hard edge to it was unmistakable. Kerri was suddenly aware of the power of his presence, his ability to take command of a scene merely by entering a room.

"I couldn't sleep." Her fingers were automatically drawing the kimono closer about her. "I had nothing to read, so I came to — to look for a book I thought I'd left in here." The small untruth came falteringly to her lips.

"I see," he said, and she knew he disbelieved her. "And have you found it?"

"No. No, I . . ."

"What was it called?"

There was a small, deadly pause. She thought, horror crawling down her spine, had he seen her with his jacket? The way she had held it to her cheek, inhaling the very special smell that was all his . . .

Now, with his eyes watching her so calmly, she was unable to think of any title whatsoever.

"It — it was just a novel," she stammered. "I don't remember the title. It had a picture of a girl with a view of boats in the background . . ."

"I'll help you look for it." His gaze took in the empty room, the thick shadows that threw some parts of it into darkness and gave others the reflection of the moonlight. "In any case, how can you possibly see without lights."

"No, please — I'm not even sure that I left it in here."

Her self-possession was ebbing so fast that she almost felt she might turn and run from the room if he persisted in questioning her about the book. Emotional claustrophobia overwhelmed her; she began to move slowly to the door, but he was nearer the doorway than she was and in three strides he was there before her.

She stopped.

"What's the matter?" he asked. "You look shaken. What's wrong, Kerri?"

The impossibility of telling him that the little scene in the clearing still rankled in her mind made her say the first thing that came into her head. She shook her head, holding herself stiff and proud. "Nothing's wrong," she said. "What are *you* doing here, anyway? Why are you still up?"

"I never go to bed before midnight," he answered shortly. "I'd just come in and was on my way along the passage to my room when I thought I heard movements in here so I came to investigate."

She found to her dismay that there was nothing she could think of to say to this man. He had only just come in . . . had only just left that woman . . .

She felt the colour suffuse her neck and creep upwards to her face, and it seemed as if all the self-consciousness of the past had combined in one enormous moment of embarrassment and diffidence.

The knowledge that this man, with his lean dark body, could inspire the most wanton longings inside her filled her with disgust. She didn't want to be attracted to Dominic Prentice. She didn't want to feel the pull of his disturbing personality. And most of all she didn't want to contemplate the sensuous consummation of that attraction that feeling his hands upon her and his lean body pressed against her's would bring . . .

The handle of the door was cool against her palm. She tried to turn it but he put his hand over her's and stopped her.

"I want to talk to you, and this is as good a time as any."

This was no scene now played for his benefit. No matter how teasing his attitude this afternoon had been in the clearing — and she knew now that that was all it *had* been, a charade on his part in which there had not been the slightest bit of truth — now, with the door closed to the world beyond and the room hazy in the moonlight, every pitiful defence that she had ever erected against this man was collapsing fast.

"Perhaps it could wait until tomorrow," she said, the old mixture of pride and stubbornness and a dozen other jumbled emotions making her withdraw from him although she longed for him to contradict her and force her to stay. "I'm very tired."

She wondered if he would override her protests, or if he would have the perspicuity to see that the apparent rejection was not a rejection at all but merely a craving for reassurance. If things got beyond her control, she told herself, she could always turn and walk away . . .

"Tired?" Dominic said. "I thought you said you were so restless you had come in here looking for a book? Come and sit down for a minute and try to relax."

"I — it was nothing." But she allowed herself to turn from the door and sink down into one of the deep easy chairs to one side of the empty fireplace. "I couldn't sleep and wandered in here . . ."

"To find a book! So you said." His smile was cryptic. He sat down in the chair opposite her. The springs creaked softly under his weight and then were still.

After moments of long-drawn-out silence, during which time she fidgeted nervously, she forced herself to say, "You said you wanted to talk to me."

He nodded. "Yes, I do. I have invited a friend of mine, a Mrs Dalny, to dinner tomorrow evening. I just wanted you to warn Jane to be on her best behaviour, and to be sure that she chooses something suitable to wear. I'm only too aware of her feelings towards Nicole — Mrs Dalny, and rely on you to speak to my niece beforehand and warn her to watch her manners."

He raised his head and his eyes in the semi-darkness were hard and questioning. "Do I make myself clear?"

Kerri nodded. "Perfectly clear, Mr Prentice."

"Good. I just wanted to make quite

certain that you both were cognizant with my wishes."

When he seemed disinclined to add anything further, Kerri stood up, and moved back to the door. "It's very late, Mr Prentice. Perhaps you'd excuse me — I can find my book in the morning . . . "

But he was already standing up to follow her. Wanting only to escape from him now, to blot out the memory of the lovely passionate woman who had met him as the boat docked, she stepped quickly into the hall and was already past the threshold when she saw with some dismay that he was following closely behind. At her door she stopped, fumbling in her haste with the handle and heard him chuckle, felt his cool fingers disengage hers from the knob and heard his deep mocking tones in her ear. "Allow me."

She realised that her face was still flushed from her encounter with him in the lounge. Then he was pushing open her bedroom door and she could feel the colour deepening in her cheeks as he stood back for her to pass. His eyes rested on the small pile of paperbacks on her bedside table, and, his movements easy and relaxed, he turned to her to say, "I thought you said you had nothing to read?"

The words contained an innuendo which had a nuance as thin as a razor-blade, but the tone of his voice gave the implication uncomfortable depths.

She turned to him in anger. "I don't know what that remark's supposed to mean," she threw back, temper rising in the way she knew so well and which so far she had managed to keep under control, "but I really don't see what it has to do with you, Mr Prentice, if I have a *hundred* books in my bedroom . . . "

"Well, merely that I was curious as to your taste in reading, Miss Matheson. What else could I mean?" He was his old mocking self again, entangling her in verbal snares. "Goodnight."

She could feel his eyes watching her as she held the door wide open, waiting for him to move away, then, almost reluctantly, withheld the inclination to slam it, violently, after him.

It would have given her infinite

satisfaction, but she knew it would also have been childish and have got her precisely nowhere.

She sat down on the bed, breathing unevenly, but presently, when she had recovered her composure, she slipped off the kimono and got back under the sheets.

9

"**T**HAT woman!" Jane's voice was full of disgust. "Honestly, Kerri, wouldn't you think Dominic would have got her out of his system by now? The last summer I spent on the island, two, no, three years ago, she was hanging around, and she's still doing it." She grimaced. "I must say she doesn't give up easily."

Kerri tried her best to look amused although she felt anything but amusement. "Well, that's entirely your uncle's affair, Jane, and nothing whatsoever to do with us."

Jane's mouth twisted. "Affair! Now you've hit the nail on the head! It's that all right, and a pretty torrid one, too, I should say, lasting all of three years. I wonder why he doesn't make an honest woman out of her and marry the wench?"

She was silent for a moment, gazing thoughtfully across the wide span of ocean. They were sitting on the terrace taking breakfast and Kerri had related to the younger girl her uncle's wishes about the forthcoming dinner-party, and how he expected, nay, demanded, that Jane be on her best behaviour. "Mind you," she went on, giving Kerri one of her knowing looks, "Mrs Dalny *is* pretty glamorous — terribly sophisticated. I think perhaps my uncle admires these qualities in a woman. Daddy has told me before how much he admired my mother, and my mother was a very beautiful woman . . . "

A tiny frown appeared between the smooth brows. "You know, Kerri, if she hadn't chosen my father, I'm sure Dominic would have married her. I've often thought that, from what I've heard, and once, when Dominic was talking about her, my mother, I mean, I caught a sort of expression on his face that made me wonder."

She broke off and Kerri sat silently watching her, not wanting to show curiosity and yet aching to know what the girl had been about to say. Jane seemed to give herself a shake, looking up and smiling wryly at her companion. "How about a swim? Morello tells me the weather people on the islands are expecting a big storm some time fairly soon, so we'd better get our swimming in while we still can."

"All right." On their way to the beach, Kerri, unable to hold it back any longer, asked, "What happened to Mrs Dalny's husband? Were they divorced or what?"

Jane shrugged. "I don't know a great deal about her, but I think he died. A few years ago, I think."

Kerri nodded, satisfied on one point. So if Dominic wanted to marry her there was really no reason why he shouldn't. Some of the gaiety went out of the sun-filled day but she tried to ignore it, swimming and sunbathing and when they got tired of that (Yes, Kerri had become to realise, one got tired of even those delightful things eventually) they walked along the palm-fringed edge of the sands and hunted for shells.

They had changed into ancient blue jeans sawn off at the knee, and halter tops, leaving their shoulders and backs free to the warm sunlight. As they separated to go into their rooms later that afternoon Jane expressed a desire to change into yet another pair of jeans for dinner, just to spite Mrs Dalny, and Kerri felt herself agreeing with her.

But she laughed, telling Jane it was no use wasting her energy on minor confrontations when she might need to reserve it for bigger battles ahead.

Jane pouted, but agreed, albeit reluctantly, and left her to go to her own room.

Kerri pulled on the white gown, the skirt full, low-necked and sleeveless. Eyeshadow and liner did wonders for her confidence, but it could not totally hide the new wistfulness in her eyes, she thought, banishing the vulnerability of her mouth with sharp, clear lines of coral lipstick.

On the island she had got into the habit of seldom bothering with make-up the light golden tan that overlaid her skin, superseding her usual pallor.

Now, with the knowledge of the other woman sitting across the table from them at dinner, she was determined to look her best. After the briefest of hesitations, she fastened the coral necklace about her slim neck, standing back to view herself in the mirror. It hung heavy on the soft material, between her breasts, outlining them in a way that at first disturbed, then suddenly pleased her.

A maid was waiting in the hall when she finally emerged from her bedroom. "The master asks that you join him on the terrace, Miss Matheson," the native girl told her, holding open the lounge door as she spoke.

The sliding glass doors leading to the wide terrace had been pushed wide open and she could hear Jane's voice, high and excited, as she told about finding the beautiful conch shell that now resided on the mantelpiece above the fireplace.

"It's such a gorgeous shade of pink, Dominic," she was saying, "I don't think I've ever found one so perfectly shaped or such a lovely colour."

Kerri took a deep breath and walked out on to the terrace. Her hands were clenched in the folds of her skirt but she appeared perfectly relaxed as she joined the assembled group.

She noticed Nicole Dalny at once.

She was poised and calm and her burnt orange silk gown with its row of tiny pearl buttons held together by loops down the front flattered every inch of her voluptuous figure.

She was standing very close to Dominic, her hand with nails improbably tipped in silver, resting intimately on his arm as she talked to him, smiling up into his face in a way that could leave no onlooker in any doubt as to their relationship.

Kerri stood unnoticed for a moment, the smile of greeting dying on her lips. Suddenly she felt deserted, bleak and alone, aching to be back with her own kind of people, back in High Linton, and away from these exotic, hothouse folk whose lives were as remote from hers as the moon was from the sun.

She should never have doubted it, she thought unhappily. This kind of life was not for the likes of her. The tragedy was that she had already given her heart, albeit unknowingly, to that hard man who stood talking to the beautiful woman hanging on his every word, dark eyes shining like diamonds in the amber glow of the hanging lamp above them.

"Kerri, you haven't met Mrs Dalny." Dominic's voice sounded beside her and she turned, smiling. They shook hands and exchanged polite murmurs, and Kerri was perfectly aware that she had been comprehensively summed up and then dismissed as of no consequence by the sparkling dark eyes of Nicole Dalny.

"Miss Matheson is here to keep Jane company during our stay on the island," explained Dominic succinctly.

The dark eyes regarded Kerri with a speculative gleam. "As a sort of governess, you mean? How nice for Jane."

She turned to Dominic, her smile revealing perfect white teeth. Her voice held such deliberate detraction that Kerri inwardly seethed.

Dominic laughed a little indulgently and, taking her arm, guided her to the far side of the terrace. Kerri heard him say, "Well, hardly that, *chérie*, although . . ."

A moment later he had come back to Kerri, and was saying, "Kerri, let me get you a drink."

She thanked him and moved over to join Jane, who was sitting near the terrace rail, sipping from a long glass of her usual fruit juice in which ice cubes tinkled as she swirled the contents around. Her eyes examined Kerri thoughtfully, and Kerri wondered if her feelings were so transparent as to have the girl wondering.

She seated herself next to Jane on the padded bench and sipped the drink Dominic brought her, helping the little knot of sudden nostalgia to unwind again, especially when Dominic in handing her the drink gave her a smile which, although restrained, contained a fair measure of approval, his eyes going to the pretty coral necklace resting against the soft white material over the swell of her breasts.

She felt a warm glow and was glad that she had worn it. It suddenly seemed a very personal thing between them, something they alone shared even in the presence of this lovely woman and her demands on Dominic . . .

She was relieved when the maid came out to tell them dinner was served.

Nicole Dalny gave a virtuoso performance over dinner, flirting with Dominic so blatantly that Kerri found she was eating her food without tasting a mouthful.

She answered Jane's remarks so inattentively that she saw the girl looking at her with a frown, and had to think quickly for a reason to explain her absentmindedness.

"The fact is, love," she whispered, so that only the other girl could hear, "I've got a bit of a headache. I think, after dinner, I'm going to make my excuses and go to bed early."

Her eyes stared across the table to where Dominic was leaning towards the lovely dark woman, paying her such close attention that somehow Kerri was embarrassed. "Do you think your uncle would mind?"

Jane grinned. "I shouldn't think he'd even notice. I might just do the same. I must say I've had about enough of *that* woman for one day."

After dinner they retired to the large lounge, where Dominic sat down before the piano and, to Kerri's surprise, began to play.

His brown fingers flew over the keys in an effortless rendering of one of Chopin's lighter pieces. Soon Nicole went over and stood next to him at the piano and, after a few minutes, when Kerri didn't think she could bear it another second, she stood and murmured in a break in the music, "Perhaps you'll excuse me, Mr Prentice. I think I'll go to bed. I — I have the beginnings of a headache."

Nicole looked up and her eyebrows rose as she darted the younger girl a look of sheer icy displeasure. "How unfortunate." Her voice was equally icy. "Perhaps you don't appreciate good music, Miss Matheson."

"Nicole!" Dominic's voice chided gently. He raised his head to look at Kerri, noting the flush on her cheeks at Nicole's words.

"I understand, Kerri. If you are not feeling well, by all means retire early. Perhaps a full day in the sun was too much for you, with your colouring."

Kerri nodded, avoiding the other woman's cold stare. "I dare say that was it."

Jane made her apologies also and the two girls went along to their rooms. Jane followed Kerri into her's, collapsing without ceremony on to the bed as she kicked off her shoes. "That woman!" she said explosively.

Kerri laughed indulgently, as Jane continued, "*I* think she wants so much to be Mrs Dominic Prentice that she'll do anything to get him."

"I was rather under the impression that she already *had* him," murmured Kerri, dryly.

Jane shrugged. "Do you think my uncle will ever marry her, Kerri? I mean, it would be disastrous if he did."

Kerri forced herself to speak steadily as she turned from those searching eyes, putting her necklace back in its drawer, "Who knows? I suppose he must marry one day and they do seem very much in love. At least I'm sure they have no illusions about each other."

Jane grimaced, then slid off the bed and, to Kerri's surprise, and secret pleasure, stopped to give her a swift kiss in passing.

"I suppose so. It's just that I'd rather have almost anyone else for an aunt — you, Kerri, for instance, would be ideal — than *her*."

Kerri was relieved when the door closed behind her and she was left alone with her thoughts, even though they were not with a feeling of being the happiest.

The next morning Dominic suggested they drive along to Maili again, to the bazaar where Jane's dresses, made up by the Indian tailor, were ready and waiting to be collected.

After paying the tailor and thanking him for the beautiful job he had done on the rather primitive sewing-machine — the dresses Jane had ordered were truly lovely and Kerri wished now she had had the sense to take Jane's offer of a loan — they were deposited by Dominic on seats under a beach umbrella, in the same café they had visited before.

Paying for their drinks, he said, "I won't be long, girls, but while I am here I might as well conclude some business that's been hanging on for some time."

His grey eyes rested on Kerri, directing his cautions to her. "Stay put and don't wander away. I don't feel like spending the rest of the daylight hours looking for you, not in this crowd."

Kerri promised they would and watched him walk away. She let herself relax in the bright sunshine, sipping her drink and absently watching the crowds passing by. After a while she became aware that Jane was no longer sitting beside her. She hadn't noticed the girl move away, and, alarmed, she sprung to her feet, placed her drink on the table before her and gazed anxiously about.

Heavens, Dominic would be *livid* if the very thing he had warned her about had been allowed to happen. Jane's shining blonde head was nowhere to be seen among the dark, frizzy heads of the crowd.

Pulses leaping with fright, she saw at that very moment Dominic's tall figure, towering above the rest of the crowd, making its way back towards her. She was surely in trouble now, she thought, Dominic's warning ringing in her ears. The very next flight out of the island and she'd be on it . . . without a doubt.

Stricken-faced, she watched as he came closer, smiling at a couple of small native children dressed in brightly coloured beads and very little else, gambolling on the sand a few paces from where she stood, nodding a greeting to an old man who paused to greet Dominic with a wide smile, as though they were old friends.

He must, she thought, know quite a few of the natives if he came back time and again to spend the summer on this lovely island . . .

But where on earth was Jane?

She dragged her eyes away from him and gazed about her, almost in desperation, wanting to run, to hide in the mass of dark-skinned people who milled around her. Useless, she knew, so, instead, she drew herself up to her full height and waited with bated breath for him to join her.

Words trembled on her lips, words of excuse, but even as she thought about them she knew he would not be interested in excuses, only in results.

She saw the warmth of his smile as he said goodbye to the old man, and braced herself for the explosion — and at the same moment Jane's voice beside her said, breathlessly, "Wow, just made it! That was lucky!"

There was no time to ask where she'd been, for Dominic was seating himself beside them at the wrought-iron table, stretching out his long legs in the sun and saying that they'd just have another drink then be on their way. They were strange days, the ones that followed. Jane had once more become quiet and morose, which Kerri put down to overtiredness as she insisted on swimming every day and nagging her uncle until he agreed to take them out at night.

Although their little jaunts were kept strictly within a time limit — by eleven o'clock they were home and in their beds — Kerri realised that too much outdoor activity, plus the nightlife, was hard to take. Especially in this latitude. It made one so lazy and indolent, one just wanted to lay about all day.

Nicole Dalny seemed to have left the island, if only for a brief time, for Kerri had overheard Dominic speaking on the phone a few days after the dinner-party, bidding her goodbye and to 'take care'.

After a while, Jane's behaviour seemed to make the atmosphere more strained than ever. Her manner remained irritable and moody, and if Kerri tried to make amends by trying to be gay, she could only expect a waspish reply.

The girl of the dinner-party, who had kissed her goodnight, had changed into the girl Kerri knew those first few weeks on the island. Nothing she said or did pleased Jane and whatever she suggested they do, the girl immediately took a delight in suggesting something different.

Dominic was too wrapped up in his work to notice the change in his niece, and Kerri didn't think it at all expedient to point it out to him.

Finally, tired of the carping tones, the fits of moodiness that were so upsetting, she said to the girl one morning, "What's with you these days? You've been an absolute drag ever since that day at the bazaar."

Immediately she said it she knew she had done the wrong thing, for Jane turned to her with that odd brilliant light shining in the dark eyes, that warned that tears were not far away, and snatching up her towel from where it lay at her feet on the sand, she snapped, "How I choose to behave has got nothing to do with you, Kerri Matheson. If I feel like being a drag that's my affair and not yours."

Kerri had long since given up trying to make any sense out of this kind of remark, but she had to admit that Jane's

164

change of mood worried her.

Where before there had been a kind of sympathy between them, especially where Nicole Dalny was concerned, now there was only tension and irritation.

Now, as Jane's fits of temper and irritability became almost unbearable, Kerri thought about the little episode when she had been missing, if only for a short time.

Had something happened to upset Jane during those minutes that afternoon she'd been away from the seafront café? If so, what? What, for heaven's sake, could have been upsetting enough to have caused such a change in Jane's attitude.

Although never particularly bosom pals, the two girls had achieved a sort of understanding in those first few weeks on the island, and now, with Jane's pettishness, everything was spoiled.

At last, as though sensing something of the situation, Dominic early one afternoon, suggested they all go swimming farther along the beach where there would be more people. This was something he seldom did, preferring their own private stretch of beach, and Jane's eyes gleamed with excitement, although her mood instantly changed when she saw how her uncle looked at Kerri as he spoke.

Kerri, too, couldn't help but notice how his eyes settled on her, almost in eagerness, as though begging her approval, and she flushed, turning her head away as Jane exclaimed, "Oh, Dominic, that would be super! Let's go where there are *lots* of people — tourists, people surfing."

Dominic nodded his head and he said with a lazy drawl, "Just give me time to get my things, then, and I'll join you by the car."

In her room Kerri caught herself humming a little tune to herself as she changed, choosing an emerald green bikini in place of the modest one-piece costume she usually wore. Against her golden tan it looked alluring, she decided, turning one way and then another to view herself in the mirror. She snatched up a white towelling coat and slipped it on. It came just down to her hips and, long legs exposed to view below the short jacket, she joined Jane outside by the waiting car.

Dominic joined them a few minutes later. He had changed into the denim jacket and trousers, as Kerri liked to see him, and carried, like the girls, a large towel.

On their way to the beach, Jane monopolised his attention, chattering about nonsensical things and turning and twisting in her seat until at last he said, in an amused voice, "Jane, stop wriggling! I declare, you're worse than a child."

"I can't help it, Dominic. I'm so excited."

Dominic looked at her with pursed mouth. "Why on earth should you be excited? We've been out quite a bit lately, it's nothing new."

"I know. It's just that — that you've never taken us to this particular stretch of beach before, and I hear the surfing here is fantastic."

Dominic grimaced, catching Kerri's eye. "Just as long as you don't expect me to give you a demonstration, I'll take your word for it."

There was quite a crowd of people at the place where they finally stopped, parking the car on the road just above the line of palms that edged the sand. The first thing Kerri saw as they spread their towels on the warm sand was the towering blondeness of the youth with whom Jane seemed to have struck up an acquaintance that day of the island trip.

Although Jane gave no indication of being aware of his presence Kerri felt she was fully conscious of his nearness.

Kerri would have been content to have lounged just where they had dropped their towels for the rest of the day. And she knew that Dominic, relaxing on his back beside her, one muscular arm resting across his eyes to shield them from the bright sun, was settled, too. But Jane was not in the mood for lying unnoticed. Putting herself firmly in the picture, she kept on to her uncle until he condescended to race her to the water.

He stirred himself reluctantly as Jane eagerly grabbed his hand and pulled him after her. At the last moment, he turned to where Kerri sat, knees drawn up to her chest, and the lazy gleam in his eyes, if not his words, drew her to her feet too.

"Come on, can't let the youngsters have all the fun."

With a high, shrill laugh, Jane turned and raced madly down the gently sloping beach to the line of surf that edged the sand. It was rougher than they expected, being used to the more gentle swell on the beach near the house, and Kerri became slightly alarmed when it seemed intent on picking her up and slamming her back on to the sand.

And then Dominic was there, swinging her around and away from the fierceness of the waves, his arms round her reassuringly. Laughing, she was too bemused by his nearness to feel any further alarm. Jane floundered nearby, watching them with narrowed eyes, before going off in the opposite direction to where a gang of youths were struggling to keep their balance on surfboards.

Watching her go, Dominic called, "Don't go out too far, Jane. It's a good deal rougher than I anticipated."

"I won't," she called back, glancing back over her shoulder at them.

After a few moments of being battered by the waves, Kerri admitted to having enough, and she and Dominic went back to their towels, relaxing in the hot sunlight with a sigh of pure pleasure.

They watched Jane's progress along the beach. In their ragged shorts and bronzed bare torsos, the young surfers were good-looking and happy; they called out greetings to Jane as she approached.

"I hope Jane doesn't try to be too daring," he observed, leaning back on one elbow as he watched them with eyes narrowed against the sun. One of the boys was endeavouring to keep his balance on a scarlet-coloured board, and not doing particularly well, and Kerri laughed as Dominic added, doubtfully, "I don't know that I care for her trying that."

"Don't worry. Jane knows what she's doing," she answered lightly. "I'm sure she wouldn't try anything foolish."

When he didn't answer, she turned her head to see that he was watching her with those mocking, half-closed eyes, a slight smile playing about his mouth.

"But you wouldn't, would you, Kerri? Try anything foolish, I mean? For example, sitting here with a crusty old bachelor while you could be having fun on the beach with those good-looking young guys."

She knew he was teasing and shook her head, quickly. "Uh — uh! I don't consider you a crusty old bachelor."

"I must say I'm flattered."

She forced herself to look away, remembering Nicole Dalny, the blatant possessiveness of the woman and how this man had lapped it up.

"You don't have to be, flattered, I mean," she murmured, hands clasped round slim ankles as she sat on the sand, "It's just that I prefer the safety of the beach to exposing myself to that rough water."

"Hm, maybe you're right."

There was a long silence during which time Kerri, lying back on her towel, found herself dozing. All this fresh air really was fatiguing to a girl, making one somnolent and drowsy, even in broad daylight . . .

Then all of a sudden Dominic was rising, starting to his feet with the fluid grace of a panther, and there were shouts from the surfers and then he was running, the short fluffy towelling jacket he wore flying open in the stiff breeze as he ran.

Kerri's blood ran cold as she realised Jane's blond head was far out to sea, struggling with the unwieldy surfboard. Her eyes flew back to the rest of the surfers. Of the tall, blond boy there was no sign.

Heart thudding wildly, she heard Dominic's voice, shouting, "Jane, don't be an idiot. Come back here."

Although he called with all his might, Kerri was sure that his voice was but a puny sound against the noise of the crashing surf. Something seemed to urge her forward, and then she was in the water, swimming strongly against its pull, out to where Jane's head was still visible against the blue-green water. Once past the heavy surf, she found it was easier and always a good swimmer, she went forward with all her might.

If only she could get up some *speed*. Her limbs soon felt stiff and awkward, already tiring in the heavy swell. And she was so cold that moving at all seemed an almighty effort. Surrounded by the creamy-topped water, she was conscious of only one thing. She had to get to Jane. She was responsible for the girl this summer — well, wasn't she . . . ? and it was up to her to save her . . .

No sooner had she had these thoughts than she began to flounder dreadfully. Her fear made her lose her sense of rhythm and she was hit by a wave and tugged under as it rose to its full height; the kind of wave the young surfers loved but which they were now watching with horror.

She began to cough agonisingly. The cold seemed to freeze her limbs and now she could do nothing but choke and fight weakly in the powerful grip of the swell.

10

THE water was all around her, in her eyes, her mouth . . .

She couldn't see Jane any more, couldn't see the beach or know what Dominic was doing . . .

There was a thunderous singing in her ears as she relaxed, suddenly weary of fighting. It was no use. One couldn't fight the ocean . . .

It seemed that she was again down in the deep Technicolor depths of the water she had explored so pleasurably all those days before. There was a heavy dark weight on her chest and her ears still rang, and her head felt as though it was bursting. Otherwise, she thought with wry speculation, I'm fine!

When she opened her eyes she found herself back on the sand, her own towel beneath her and a caustic Dominic kneeling beside her.

"Well, that was a brilliant thing to do, I must say," he told her with just the right inflexion of disgust in his voice. "You little fool, you almost drowned."

She pushed herself up with a painful gasp, the memory of those terrifying moments shooting through her and saw Jane sitting nearby with Dominic's towelling jacket wrapped about her.

She was shivering, gazing along the stretch of beach with a wild look that had nothing to do with her recent experience in the sea.

Her eyes were fixed on the small group of youths who stood huddled together, holding their surfboards to them like medieval knights might hold their shields, in a strangely defensive way.

Before she had time to notice anything more, Dominic, taking Kerri's hands, was pulling her to her feet, saying, some of the anger gone from his voice and anxiety taking its place, "We'd better get you two home and into a hot bath. The wind's turned quite chilly. Don't want you down with colds, do we? Not in our last few days on the island."

With a tenderness that was as disquieting as it was unexpected, he wrapped Kerri's towel round her shivering form, and calling to Jane, assisted her back to where the car was parked under the palms.

"Do you think you can hold out until we get back to the house?" he asked her, his face still pale and taut with worry.

"Of course I can," she smiled thinly, through chattering teeth. "I'm perfectly all right now."

Which wasn't entirely true, but something in the haggard way Dominic looked at her made her want to reassure him.

Jane, a dripping, forlorn figure, followed meekly behind. In the car, he observed the two girls with narrowed eyes. "What happened, for God's sake? One minute Jane's acting the fool with those boys, the next you're dashing madly out into the water in some idiot attempt to dissuade her from going out farther. There was really no need for it, Kerri. I'd already noticed and was calling her to come back."

Kerri, huddled in the towel, teeth chattered even more as the cool breeze of later afternoon wafted into the car windows. Noticing this, Dominic wound up the windows as she answered, "I don't know *what* got into me. Jane was in difficulties and I thought . . . "

Jane grimaced wryly. She uttered a short, terse word that had her uncle raising his eyebrows reprovingly. "I wasn't in difficulties," she said. "I knew perfectly well what I was doing."

"Well, it certainly didn't look like it." Kerri's voice was hot with indignation. "Who were you trying to impress? Those guys with the surfboards?"

"Does it really matter?" Dominic gazed from one to the other, frowning in exasperation. "We can discuss this later. All we really have to worry about right now is getting you into some dry clothes with a hot drink inside you."

At the house he escorted the girls to their bedrooms, depositing Jane in hers first. Pushing the girl firmly inside, he said, "Have a hot bath, then get into bed and stay there until morning. I'll have a meal and a glass of hot milk sent in to you."

Kerri, her lids heavy with fatigue, didn't need telling twice when they stopped at her door. Going into the bathroom, she ran a steaming bath and stripped off the damp towel and skimpy green bikini and left them laying on the tiled floor as she soaked in the bath.

She was pulling on one of her heavier nightgowns, for outside the wind had increased in vigour and the palm trees she could see through the bedroom window were bending under its force, when there was a soft knock on her door and one of the maids entered with a covered tray.

Hot soup, crusty rolls and fruit, with a tall glass of steaming milk laced with brandy to one side of the silver tray.

Sitting propped up on her pillows, she dined quietly, listening to the distant howl of the wind, the surf as it crashed against the island's shore. It was a depressing sound and it made Kerri all the more aware of the deep silence inside the house.

Had Dominic, weary with his niece's childish tricks and Kerri's equally puerile actions in thinking Jane was in danger and her ludicrous performance in trying to save her, had he gone out?

If Nicole Dalny had arrived back on the island, well, Kerri was sure that she would be infinitely more appealing, in the circumstances, than her own wet and bedraggled appearance and Jane's pouting demeanour.

The following morning the island woke to rain. It was streaming down the window-panes in the big lounge, and by lunchtime it had developed into a tropical storm, something most unusual for this time of the year, Dominic explained.

As Kerri stood, gazing out onto the dreary scene; garden and seafront grey with mist caused by the drifting squalls from the ocean, Dominic had joined her.

"Just as well we had that last day on the beach when we did," he exclaimed. "Imagine going out in this weather!"

Kerri grimaced. She couldn't imagine. Somehow the rain would always seem much more depressing in a setting such as this to what she was used to in High Linton. She was relieved that he was treating her like he had always done, her foolhardy behaviour of yesterday already relegated to the past.

She wanted no emotional entanglements, even a lighthearted flirtation that Jane seemed to think her quite crazy for not accepting, and which she might at one time, have enjoyed with someone as good-looking as Dominic.

But she realised with a new maturity that every relationship carried its own risks and that she had done well to hold herself aloof, as she had promised herself she would on arriving on this fascinating island.

Besides, there was that other woman . . .

Kerri was suddenly aware of him gazing at her profile and she started visibly as he said, "How about some coffee? I could do with a cup, couldn't you?"

"All right. I'll make it."

The servants had retired to their quarters after serving an early lunch and the kitchen, she knew, would be empty.

He grinned. "I thought you'd never offer."

They sat at opposite ends of the large white table in the spotless kitchen, and although Kerri searched frantically for something to say to break the silence, a subject in which they might both be interested, her mind refused to come up with anything.

The only thing she could think of was the little scene that day in the clearing. She wondered if he was thinking about it, too, or whether he hadn't given it a second thought. She was glad, when, rising, he took his cup to the stainless steel sink unit and washed it under the tap, afterwards turning it upside down on the draining-board.

Seeing she had also finished, he came over and took hers, and repeated the operation. They wandered out into the passage and, surprisingly, halfway along, he pushed open a door, pausing to look at her.

"Come into my study," he said, and with only the briefest hesitation she did as he bid.

It was an order, and when Dominic Prentice spoke like that, one obeyed. He followed her in and walked past her to switch on the big electric fire, for the air in the room was damp and cold.

Looking about her, she smiled and said, "I thought this was the inner sanctum where no mortal feet ever trod."

"I've decided to make an exception in

your case," he grinned back.

Kerri looked round in surprise. "It's no wonder you won't let anyone come in here," she said, before she could stop herself. "I've never seen such chaos in my whole life."

It was a very large room with a great deal of wood panelling, mostly of split bamboo, which she thought looked very attractive against the vividly patterned curtains of olive green, orange and white.

Several large bookcases lined the walls, all of which were filled to overflowing. Scattered around in complete disarray were sheets of typed paper, spilling on to the floor in places.

The only neat area was a large desk under the window with a typewriter and wire baskets, again filled with pages of manuscript.

"My latest epic," explained Dominic, following her gaze. "I just cannot seem to get on with it. Everything's in a muddle." He sighed. "I shouldn't have been so eager to offer to have Jane for the summer, I guess."

Kerri frowned. "Don't blame the girl for your own disorientations. Be fair and admit that Jane hasn't bothered you all that much."

Not nearly as much as your glamorous night visitor, she thought spitefully, unable to suppress the thought.

She walked over to the typewriter and stood looking down at the partly typed paper it held, while Dominic bent to gather a sheaf of papers from the floor. He rifled them into a neat package on the top of the desk, and placed them in the wire basket with the pile of others.

"Isn't there anything I can do?" she asked. "I mean, it's such a rotten day and Jane seems to have found something to occupy her time in her own room, so why can't I help you with all this?" She looked about her as she spoke, taking in the spilled papers.

He looked at her with those dark grey eyes in a way she was beginning to know so well, and smiled that slow, rare smile. "Please yourself," he said amicably. "You can stay if you like, as long as you don't incessantly chatter or peer over my shoulder."

Kerri retired in silence to the far end of the room and knelt on the floor. There were a great many pages of manuscript, on the early history of Lessane, she saw, glancing through some of them. She began to put them together, reading until she became so interested that she forgot the rain lashing at the wide picture window, and the sound of the surf thundering on the beach.

The warmth of the room took over. After a while she didn't even notice the sound of Dominic tapping out a staccato rhythm on the typewriter.

After a while, when she had picked up all the papers and placed them together neatly to one side of her, she sat back on her heels and just watched him. The quick, sure movements of his fingers were mesmerising and the light from the Anglepoise lamp he had switched on beside his typewriter struck reddish highlights from his hair.

She had slept badly the previous night, laying awake for hours before falling into a restless sleep, subjecting herself to the most prolonged bout of self-examination she had ever conducted. And the answers she had come up with made her more bewildered than ever.

So much for her casual words to Jane concerning her feelings for Dominic, she thought bitterly. Her feelings had shown her just how vulnerable she was as a woman . . .

His voice brought her back to earth with a bump. "You are one of the first women I've met who can actually keep quiet for more than five minutes," he said, stretching gracefully.

Kerri got up and walked to the fire, holding her hands out to its warmth.

"Cold?"

She shook her head, turning her face to find that, disconcertingly, he was watching her. Her colour rose and the trite remark she had been about to make about the weather died on her lips.

Wonderingly, her eyes searched his face, marking the strongly arched eyebrows above those impenetrably grey eyes, and the hard lines of his mouth and jaw. In that room, warmed by the brightness of the electric fire, the gusty, whining rain driven by wind from the ocean safely outside, her heart started thudding in a kind of ridiculous panic. The realisation came to her that she had been guilty of staring, especially when he said, and this time there was no mistaking the satirical note in his voice, "Kerri, I think you should go and make more coffee."

Hurriedly she left the room, first placing the neat piles of paper in the wire basket he indicated, and went down the passage to the kitchen while her legs still had the strength to hold her up.

Making the coffee took a long time, because her hands seemed to have acquired a tremor and her mind was still with the man in that quiet, warm room, sitting behind his desk filled with typed paper.

At last it was done, though, and after taking several deep breaths she made her way back to Dominic.

He was standing with his back to the room, gazing through the window, and as she handed him his coffee she was glad to see that her hands were relatively steady again. Glancing round at the now tidy room, he said, solemnly, "Thank you. That's the neatest I can remember this room looking for many a day. Emma used to help me keep my natural untidiness under control, but lately I guess it's got out of hand again. At one time . . . " He broke off abruptly and turned away, back to the scene outside the window.

She floundered a little. "Emma?"

"Yes. Emma was Jane's mother. We were — very close. I'm surprised at Jane not discussing such a succulent little titbit with you. She usually adores gossip in all its forms."

Under the powder blue cardigan she had slipped on her shoulders stiffened. "We do have other things to talk about, Mr Prentice." She looked at him defiantly, challenging the mockery in his eyes.

"Tut-tut! Temper again!"

"You know perfectly well what I mean," she said, her cheeks hot.

He laughed. "Why is it that we always revert to crossing swords with each other whenever we're alone for more than a few minutes? And why, for heaven's sake, must you insist on calling me Mr Prentice? The name is Dominic."

Without waiting for her reply he turned away, placing his cup on the top of the desk. "Anyway, thank you again for getting this room back into shape. I *do* appreciate it even if you don't think I do."

She looked down at the carpet. "Don't mention it. Now, I think I ought to go and check on Jane. See how she's feeling."

"You never thought to tell me how *you* are feeling," he broke in, gazing at her curiously. "Or even *why* you made that brave, but rather foolish, dash into the water to rescue Jane."

Her eyes didn't lift from the carpet.

"Well," he said, "I'm waiting for an answer."

"I don't have an answer," she told him, almost defiantly. "I just thought that Jane was in trouble and, after all, you have hired me for the summer to keep an eye on her."

"But not to risk your life for her foolishness."

"Yes, well . . . I must go . . . " Carrying her cup, she went out, closing the door gently behind her, hearing his soft chuckle as she went.

She felt her cheeks glow warmly as she went along the passage and back to the kitchen. His words rang in her ears, "Why is it that we revert to crossing swords . . . "

She was thankful that he had let her go so easily. A brisk walk along the beach might be just what she needed to clear her head. She saw that the rain had stopped and the sky on the horizon was clearing rapidly, making way for another spectacular sunset.

She tapped gently at Jane's bedroom door, then when there was no reply, opened it and peered in. The girl might be sleeping, after her experience of the day before. To her surprise, and annoyance, Jane wasn't in the room.

The maid who was busy opening all the bedroom windows after the rain said she had no idea where she had gone.

The girl, to Kerri's trepidation, was nowhere to be found, and after fruitless moments of hesitation, calling the girl's name and searching the bedrooms and kitchen, peering unsuccessfully out on to the flooded terrace, Kerri decided Dominic would have to be told.

As she spoke his mouth tightened, his eyes narrowing in a cold stare.

"She isn't anywhere? You're sure?"

Kerri nodded. "Quite sure, Mr Prentice — Dominic," remembering his admonishment about not using his given name. She went on, "None of the staff has seen her, at least not in the past hour, and I've looked everywhere."

"Are you sure she's not in the kitchen? Perhaps we were not the only ones who felt the need for a cup of coffee."

"I've looked. But we can look again . . . "

She followed Dominic out of the room and, between them, they checked all the rooms. Dominic threw a raincoat about his shoulders and ventured out on to the terrace, but this, too, was empty. Foolish to think she might be there, anyway, Kerri mused, in this weather . . .

"It isn't possible for her to be too far away," said Dominic, wiping the rain from his face with his handkerchief. "Besides, Jane hates the rain. She would not go out in it unless she was forced to."

Involuntarily they both looked out at the still tossing ocean under the lightening sky, the palm trees bent almost double by the wind, and each felt the first tiny tremors of fear stir inside them.

"You don't suppose . . . " Kerri began, then checked herself. "No, I'm sure that's not the answer . . . "

"Suppose what?" he asked impatiently.

"I was just wondering if she could have asked Morello to drive her to town, or to the hotel. Perhaps to meet some friends . . . "

"Jane has no friends on the island. Certainly none that either I or her father would approve of." Watching Kerri's face, seeing the uncertainty there, he paused, then went on with some reluctance, "Well, I suppose there's a chance that she *did* get Morello to take her somewhere. Although, if he has, without informing me, he'll soon be finding himself another job."

"Anyway, it's worth a try," Kerri said, following him as he turned to the telephone. She knew that Morello had living quarters over the garage and was connected by the intercommunication phone.

But the man denied any knowledge of Jane's whereabouts, sounding as troubled as Dominic over the hissing wires.

Dominic gave orders that he come over to the house immediately, bringing the car. To Kerri he explained, "Do you really think there is a likelihood that Jane may have gone to the hotel?"

Helplessly, Kerri stared at him. "I don't know what to think, Dominic. As you've warned me more than once, your niece is very impulsive. She likes her own way . . ."

"Go and fetch a coat and get in the car." He sounded so irritable that Kerri felt her anger flair. He acted as though it was *her* fault that Jane was missing, when they both knew that once the girl had made up her mind there was little anyone could do to stop her.

"I'm sorry, Dominic. One can't watch someone twenty-four hours a day . . ."

"I wouldn't expect you to." He glared at her. "Don't be an idiot. I'm not blaming you."

"I'll get my coat," she murmured, suitably subdued.

A few minutes later they were leaving the flooded driveway and turning on to the main highway towards the hotel.

The heavy downpour had turned the countryside into a quagmire and the verges of the road were pitfalls of muddy water. The sky to the west, although lightening, was magnificent with ribbons of scarlet and flame, reaching down to a still grey ocean, and Kerri shivered inwardly, knowing darkness could not be far away.

She prayed that the rain would not start again, that they would get to the hotel in one piece, for the way Morello was driving, avoiding the mud-holes as best he could, was crazy in the extreme.

Peering through the windows, she thought; 'But how would the girl, supposing she *had* got as far as the hotel, how would she *get* there? Walking? In this weather? You must be joking, Kerri girl! Hitch-hiking? That would be the obvious answer. Most of her generation thought nothing of thumbing a lift.'

Morello said nothing, but sat crouched over the wheel, shoulders haunched as though blaming himself for Jane's absence, obviously dreading Dominic's wrath.

Then they were driving into the

entrance of the hotel. The car-park was almost empty. "Stay there," Dominic ordered, turning to look at Kerri as he, followed by Morello, climbed out of the car. "I'll go in and check if she's there or if anyone's seen her. Morello can question the rest of the staff."

She sensed that he wanted to be alone, so she sat quietly and waited for his return. It was all too soon, and even from where she sat she could guess that he had drawn a complete blank.

"Nothing," he said wearily, as he got back in beside her. "The reception desk is positive they haven't seen her, and they admit remembering her, and you, from your previous visits. I had a waitress check all the ladies' rooms. She wasn't there."

For a long moment he sat, staring thoughtfully at the chauffeur's back. "Morello checked in the dining-room and the nightclub, but it was no-go."

"Could she have gone somewhere else?" Kerri asked, almost desperately.

"She could have chosen a dozen places to visit. If she'd been enterprising enough to take a taxi, or got a lift, she could have gone almost anywhere on the island."

"Even in weather like this?" Kerri's voice was hesitant and he looked at her frowningly. He shook his head, the dark hair under the lurid lights that festooned the front of the hotel; red, green, gold, caught and reflected the drops of rain that hung there. "As I said before, Jane hates the rain, but if she'd really made up her mind, and, heaven forbid, had arranged to meet someone clandestinely, then it would take more than a rainstorm to stop her."

"Then what do you suggest we do?" Kerri's voice shook, and he turned his head briefly, to look at her. "There are three possibilities," he said. "First, we've arrived here too early, and if we wait she'll come walking in any moment now. Secondly, she has no intention of coming here but is headed elsewhere, which can mean anything. And thirdly, we're making a great ballyhoo about nothing and there is a simple explanation."

As he spoke, Morello turned in his seat to look at them. "The first and the last possibilities I'll accept, Mr Prentice," he said, "but the second one I cannot.

195

How would Miss Jane *get* to wherever she was going in the first place? If she phoned for a taxi, surely someone in the house would have overheard, or seen her leaving?"

"Then let's be a little constructive," Kerri blurted out, unable to stop herself. "Shouldn't we call the police?"

"I don't think there's very much they can do, Kerri," said Dominic. "She's not been missing long enough to call them in. Besides, think what fools we'd look if she *has* just been visiting someone we don't know about . . . What's wrong?"

Kerri had remembered something and was staring at him with wide eyes. "I've just thought of something," she murmured, hesitantly, "a boy she was talking to on the island that day we saw the fire-walkers . . . "

"And?" he made in impatient gesture.

"She was with him when I went to fetch her to board the boat," Kerri explained. "I thought there was something familiar about him, now I've just remembered, I saw him first that time you were away and Morello took us to the bazaar at Maili. Then yesterday, when we arrived on that beach, he was there again with the surfers."

"And you think she made an assignation with him to meet him again?"

Dominic was glaring at her, mouth a thin line, betraying how firmly he was trying to conceal his anger.

Again Kerri hesitated. "I don't know, Dominic . . . they seemed very interested in each other and your niece is a very attractive and lively girl. The boy," she added, quickly, seeing how Dominic's mouth hardened even more, "if it's any consolation, seemed a good sort, pleasant and well-mannered. I imagine him to be an American."

"Why didn't you tell me about him before this?"

"There was nothing to tell, Dominic. She'd only seen him very briefly and there was certainly no indication that she was making a date to see him again, or anything like that. And yesterday, he didn't stay long . . .

"Humph!" He turned away. "And you have no idea, I suppose, where this young Apollo could be found?"

"I'm sorry." Helplessly she looked at

him, at the tension that showed clearly on his face. The drive back to the house was a silent one and as they drew up before the front door, Kerri watched the entrance, hoping against hope that Jane would come running out to meet her.

But her hopes were dashed when, once in the house, the maids said they had continued their search and she was still not to be found.

11

MOROSELY, she followed Dominic along the passage to his study, equally morose, Morello drove the car round to the garage.

Once in his room, Dominic lifted the telephone and spoke to the local police station. Replacing the receiver, he looked at Kerri and said, "The Sergeant says they will keep a look-out for her, but we mustn't worry too much. Teenagers vanish every day of the week but seldom for more than a few hours. They are usually found on the beach, with a gang of other kids, surfing or listening to someone playing a guitar."

"How very comforting," Kerri said, miserably. "You really think Jane could be doing that? After the rainstorm we've just had?"

He shrugged. "There's really not much we can do but wait, Kerri."

Suddenly he smiled. "How about

another cup of coffee? It might be a long wait."

"If you like."

It was undoubtedly one of the most uncomfortable and distressing hours in Kerri's life. Dominic kept insisting that he didn't consider it her fault in Jane's disappearance, but she felt very differently. If she hadn't hung around with him in that warm, comfortable, if untidy room, sorting papers and adoring him with her eyes, Jane would not now be missing, causing the police to scurry around the island, looking for her.

After she had brought a second cup of coffee, Dominic didn't say a word, which added considerably to her discomfort. She should have seen that the girl would have done something like this, for with her abrupt and upsetting change of mood she knew Jane was in a state of mind to do *anything* . . .

Without her realising it, Dominic must have been studying her, for suddenly he said, gently, "Look, you mustn't blame yourself for this, you know. Jane is at an age when the spur of the moment is much more important than anyone's feelings. I've already told you, it isn't your fault."

"I know you're trying to spare my feelings, Dominic," she said, shivering a little, "but I was hired to look after her and didn't. It's as simple as that."

Coming over to where she sat, he took both her hands in his and said, concern in his voice, "You're freezing! How about another cup of coffee?"

His voice trailed off as she gave a shaky laugh, grimacing. "I don't think so, Dominic. If I drink another cup of coffee I think I'll explode."

He grinned. He was so close to her that she could smell the dampness of his clothes, and she had a strong desire to bury her face in the warmth of his shoulder and just cry, which was ridiculous when she considered that she hadn't cried for years. At least not since she was fourteen and her puppy was run over outside their house and killed.

Just in time she realised that her feelings had little to do with Jane's disappearance, and with a violent jerk, moved away from temptation, withdrawing her hands, remembering again that misty green clearing and the brush of his lips against hers . . .

"I'm all right, really. I think I'll go to my room and get another cardigan, this one is a little damp," she told him, still shivering but not entirely because she was cold.

"All right," he said. His lips twisted wryly as though he, too, recalled the little scene in the clearing and the way she had also pushed him away, then.

He turned back to his desk, beginning to rifle through a sheaf of papers in a wire basket. "While you're along that way, would you mind going into my room and getting me a dry shirt? This one feels decidedly damp. You'll find them in the top drawer of the dresser beside the bed."

She went along the passage to her room and changed into a bright cherry red sweater, the colour of which gave a warm glow to the darkening day. His bedroom was farther along the passage. It was a large room, on the opposite side of the corridor from hers and Jane's, facing the back gardens, and surprisingly tidy after the chaos in his study.

Watercolours of local scenes hung on the wall and she stopped under one to examine the signature.

Nicole Dalny!

Well, she thought, say what you like about the lady, but she certainly had talent — one way or another! The painting was exquisite, the colours of the ocean almost transparent, as though viewed through crystal glass, the sky a cloudless blue from horizon to horizon.

Dominic's bed was huge, King-size, covered with a neatly tucked in bedspread of Indian cotton that matched the curtains. In front of the large picture window was a cane chair made comfortable with brightly coloured cushions. Kerri could imagine him sitting there in the evenings, perhaps smoking, musing over his current book.

It was the wrong time to be thinking of such things, she told herself sternly, and turned away, to the large chest of drawers that almost filled the space between his bed and the window. Opening the top drawer, she found a neat pile of shirts, and picked up one and left the room.

In his study, Dominic was pouring

himself a brandy from the cut-glass decanter he kept on the small table by the fireplace. He turned at her entrance, holding out his glass invitingly. "You said you'd had enough coffee. How about a drink, then?"

Kerri shook her head and handed him the shirt. "No, thanks, Dominic. I'm not really a drinking person."

He grinned, busily unbuttoning the shirt he had on. "So I've noticed!" and she knew he was thinking of the drink he had offered her that time in the clearing and its consequences. Before she could think up a reply, he added, "Not even at a time like this, Kerri?"

Again she shook her head, and with an effort dragged her gaze away from the brown, muscular chest revealed by the open shirt. Of course, she had seen him in his bathing costume, she told herself, but somehow this seemed so much more intimate, here, in this quiet room, with the rest of the house silent . . .

"No, thanks." With a great effort, she managed to keep her voice from shaking.

He shrugged and slipped the shirt

from his shoulders. Pensively, he slid his arms into the sleeves of the fresh shirt, unhurriedly, looking at her, and she thought with a flash of irritation; he's doing it on purpose! He's doing it to tease me . . .

It was not merely the ruthlessness she sensed in his personality that troubled her, it was this physical power that he possessed, and the knowledge that he had the assurance to make her feel this way.

He walked unhurriedly across the room towards her, his fingers busy with the small pearl buttons on the fresh shirt. He came to a halt and stood looking down at her, and again she was aware of the magnetic personality of the man, of the grey brilliance of his eyes as they searched hers, and the soft rose of her cheeks heightened and betrayed her.

Almost reluctantly, she turned her head away, embarrassed that he should be able to read her mind. She said, her voice shaking so badly now that he grinned, "Shouldn't you phone the police again, just in case they've heard something . . . ?"

He shrugged and turned away, as

though satisfied at the turmoil he had produced in her. "The local police can handle this sort of thing far more efficiently than we can, Kerri, without us getting under their feet. I know the Sergeant well enough to know he is an extremely thorough man and will do anything in his power to trace Jane. Meanwhile, as I said before, the best thing we can do is sit quiet and wait for either news of her or for her to turn up on her own. Unfortunately, waiting is one of the most difficult things to do in these circumstances."

"Would you rather I left you, Dominic — went to my room?"

"No. Let's say I'm getting used to your company."

After that there was little to say. Conversation seemed both unnecessary and pointless and after a while, as the late afternoon became darker and a fresh breeze took the place of the wild wind that had plagued the island all day, and still no news came from the local police, they sat and tried to pretend that everything was fine.

By nightfall the rain had ceased. The

moon was rising, a deep amber gold against the blue sapphire sky. Its track lay across the water like a broad rippling beam and in the light of it Kerri saw wreckage from the pitifully wretched homes of the islanders. The anguished cries of the villagers were mute now and the silence that surrounded the island seemed vast and empty. The loneliness was almost unbearable.

It was almost ten o'clock, and Kerri had found herself dozing in the warm, comfortable room, when they caught the faint sounds of a car engine in the front driveway. Dominic raised his head abruptly, glanced sharply at Kerri, and then got to his feet with a rapidity that turned the action into a soft blur of movement.

Kerri followed him slowly to the front door, where an anxious-looking maid was standing, gazing wide-eyed into the darkness. For a moment they stood waiting, saying nothing, until the headlights of the car swung round the curve of the drive and came to a halt directly in front of them.

It was the police car and Kerri found

herself praying, "Oh, dear God, don't let anything have happened to her . . . " when Dominic strode forward, just as the door of the driver's side swung open and a dark, bulky figure got out.

"'Evening, Mr Prentice," said a deep voice. "We thought you might like something that belongs to you."

The man bent, opened the back door and stood waiting. Almost immediately Jane got out. Damp and unnaturally subdued, she stood before her uncle, gazing at him with wide and, Kerri couldn't help but notice, frightened eyes.

Dominic didn't move, and even from where she waited in the open doorway, Kerri could feel his cold fury.

With tight lips, he at last said, "Get inside. I'll deal with you later."

Jane walked slowly to where Kerri waited, and the older girl slipped an arm about her, an unconscious movement that Jane seemed to appreciate. Without a word Kerri drew the slim figure inside, and towards the lounge, where, for the first time since her arrival, someone had lit a fire in the wide stone fireplace. She gave the girl a little push, saying, "Sit down, love. We were so worried . . . "

Dominic's even, controlled voice came from behind them. Striding into the room, he didn't even wait until Kerri had closed the door behind him before he began to speak. With devastating effectiveness he said what he had to say while Jane sat huddled in one corner of the largest settee, looking pale, and yet, somehow, defiant.

Her eyes were unflinchingly fixed on his, and Kerri could tell by her quick breathing that the girl was as scared as she herself was, yet she didn't show it. At last, when he'd finished saying all he had to say, Dominic ground out, "Now you can go to your room and change out of those damp things. I'll listen to any explanations you care to give me afterwards."

Jane moved very quickly, too quickly for him to see the tears that Kerri glimpsed as she passed through the doorway. For a moment she thought Dominic was going to say something else, but he seemed to change his mind and allowed her to go without further admonishment.

Kerri looked at him and after the girl had gone, said, "She *is* nearly grown-up, Dominic. You didn't have to be so hard on her."

Dominic did not reply so she said nothing else. Because she knew, now, by the drawn, tight look about his mouth that his words had not been prompted by anger, but by fear. The sort of fear that makes a mother give a wayward child a sharp slap when its been lost in a shop and she at last finds it.

The Sergeant was waiting outside and as though suddenly realising this, Dominic hurried out to find him. He explained how they had come to find Jane, saying, "We should, of course, have thought of it at once, only I wouldn't have believed anyone would have been so crazy to be out after that rainstorm. My man had already searched the nearest beaches, and reported no sign of your niece, but when the rain cleared up I got to thinking about the shack the kids sometimes make use of at the western end of the island. It's very deserted and not many people use it any more, apart from the kids. Well, I drove along that way and, believe it or not, my hunch paid off. There were about a dozen young people there, dancing to someone's portable record-player, and they'd lit a fire and were having a barbecue. They all looked a little resentful when I poked my nose in, but your niece immediately gave herself away by running outside, through a back entrance of the shack. I caught up with her and when at last she admitted who she was I brought her back."

Looking at him, he made it sound so easy, thought Kerri, when he probably had a very irascible young lady on his hands.

Frowningly, Dominic asked, "Was there anyone with her?"

The man looked puzzled. "With her, sir? Maybe a dozen or so kids, as I mentioned . . . "

"No, I mean actually with her. A boy . . . ?"

"I didn't see anyone that seemed to be actually *with* your niece, sir, but when she saw me she moved so fast it would be difficult to say whether she was or not."

Dominic moved forward and held out

his hand. "Thank you, Sergeant Knowles. I appreciate your help. Now, if you will excuse me . . . ?"

Taking the hint, the Sergeant shook hands and turned back to the car. About to depart, he leaned from the driver's window to say, "Young people these days don't realise just how worried we get about them. They think just because *they* feel confident and in complete control of the situation, everything must be all right. Even so, sir, it seemed to be pretty harmless fun they were having, so I shouldn't be *too* hard on the young lady if I were you."

Tightly, Dominic said, "Thank you, Sergeant. I'm grateful for your advice."

When the man had at last gone, Dominic turned to Kerri. After giving her a sharp look, he murmured, "You look all in. Why don't you go to bed?"

"Not yet, Dominic. For one thing, I know I wouldn't be able to sleep."

He frowned, hearing something in her voice that sounded faintly like disapproval. With a sigh he led the way back to the lounge, then seated himself to one side of the blazing fire, and looked at her. "All right, out with it. You didn't agree with what I said to Jane, is that it? How do *you* think I should have handled it, patted her on the back and told her she was a good girl?"

"No, of course not. Of course you had to lecture her. She gave us all a very nasty fright and it didn't seem to bother her in the least. But you *were* a little hard on her, Dominic. She *is* young and needs company of her own age."

He frowned, his hands reaching for the silver table lighter nearby. He seldom smoked and Kerri noticed how his hands trembled, very slightly, as he lit his cigarette. Replacing the lighter on its table, he gazed thoughtfully at the thin drift of smoke rising from his cigarette, and said, "I thought that was the reason you were here — to supply Jane with company of her own age."

She gave a short laugh. "I'm flattered, but besides being a few years older than Jane, I'm also the wrong sex."

"You mean, she really is taking an interest in boys?" He nodded before she could answer. "Yes, of course. You mentioned the young surfer. I'll have to watch that in future."

He broke off abruptly, then added, "I'm glad you were here, Kerri. It isn't easy to cope with something like this when the child is not your own."

It wasn't so easy to cope with him, either, she thought, seeing the way he was looking at her. She got to her feet and said, briskly, "Well, I think I will go to bed, after all, if you don't mind, Dominic. I really am tired. Goodnight."

Wearily he got to his feet. The half-smoked cigarette spun in a slow arch and fell into the golden red flames. "Goodnight, Kerri."

12

SHE saw Jane at breakfast the next morning and she behaved as though the entire episode had never happened. No signs of strain showed on her face or in her clear eyes and Kerri thought it wisest to forget the whole thing, relate it to the past and not refer to it again. Their relationship was very tenuous and delicate at the best of times, and she knew the best way to destroy it completely would be to reintroduce the subject of yesterday.

Whether Dominic wanted to or not was his privilege.

Dominic joined them this morning and they ate in silence, Jane seeming intent on finishing as quickly as possible and getting away from the two of them.

Breakfast over, to Kerri's surprise, however, Jane accepted her invitation to walk on the beach. They trudged along the waterline, gingerly side-stepping the larger breakers, and Kerri rejoiced to see the faint pink return to the pale cheeks and know the worst was over. They walked barefoot, seeking treasure trove thrown up by the sea during the storm: shells, fantastically shaped pieces of wood and yards of bubbly seaweed. The booty presented itself to them in a continual line at the water's edge.

After a long silence, Kerri said, "I'd promised myself I wasn't going to bring this up again, Jane, but don't you feel like telling me why you did it? Your uncle was really worried. If you could have just seen him . . ."

The girl pursed her lips and looked away, seawards. "Big deal!"

Her voice held derision. "I can't see him getting worried about anything, except maybe his old books. He and my father are the same where I'm concerned." She stopped and bending down lifted a particularly intriguing piece of wood, turning it this way and that in her hand. "God, everything's such a drag. There's just nothing to do in this place and yet when I *do* find someone who is interested in me having a bit of fun, Dominic acts as if I'm the devil's own

216

daughter, to say the least."

"I don't suppose your uncle would have minded so much if you'd told us first you were going out," Kerri pointed out quickly.

The girl's lips curled with disbelief. "And he would have let me go?"

When Kerri hesitated Jane gave a short laugh and said, "No, of course he wouldn't, and you know it."

She shot an oblique glance at Kerri. "Don't *you* get so bored you could scream? You're not all that much older than me and it must be just as much a drag for you, here on the island."

"You forget that I'm here doing a job. That your uncle pays me to keep an eye on you."

Jane's laughter rang out, shrill, startling a pair of seabirds fighting over something farther along the beach. "Didn't do very well yesterday, then, did you? Was my uncle very angry with you, Kerri? When he spoke to me like he did I thought at first I would die. It's fortunate that I'm resilient and soon get over such things."

As much as she tried, Kerri could not

hide the smile the girl's words conjured up. She said, "Did you really go out to meet that boy? That blond guy I saw you with after the fire walkers that day."

Jane nodded, an impish grin lifting the corners of her mouth. "How did you know? I thought we were doing a pretty good job at concealing it."

"Not good enough, Jane. I guessed he might have something to do with your sudden and inexplicable behaviour."

"Did you — tell my uncle?"

Kerri looked at her thoughtfully. "I mentioned it briefly in passing, but he didn't seem to put much reliance on what I said, and I did add that it was purely guesswork on my part."

For a moment she thought she saw someone much older than the sixteen-year-old peer at her from behind Jane's long lashes. "Mm . . . "

"It still doesn't explain why you were prepared to risk your uncle's anger, or even why you wanted to go out in the first place. Especially in this weather."

"*I* didn't know it was going to rain, did I? I mean, it's not supposed to this time of year. And I'd already promised

Mark I'd meet him." She took a deep breath and the look in her eyes became so haunting that Kerri suddenly felt deep pity for the girl. "Oh, Kerri," her cry seemed to come from the heart, "when I saw him the other day at the beach café, when we were waiting for Dominic, I couldn't help it but I ran after him. I realised afterwards how childish I was acting, especially when I saw he was with another girl. He was walking with his arm about her waist and they were laughing about something. He didn't see me, but I just wanted to die. Then, the other day, when he was on that beach Dominic took us to, with the surfers, I met him again and he told me all about his sister and I realised that was the other girl he'd been walking with. He said he'd been thinking about me ever since he first saw me, and he asked where I lived . . . "

She bit her lip, watching Kerri's face to see how she was taking it.

"He — he said he'd pick me up, that he had a car, and he'd take me to this place where all the kids met — if I could get permission from my uncle."

"Which, of course, you should have done but didn't."

"Oh, Kerri, don't you start. I feel badly enough about it as it is."

Kerri's lips twitched. "I can't say it notices, Jane. So that is why you were in such a filthy temper because you saw this Mark with another girl?"

Jane nodded. "Yes. I'm sorry, Kerri. You've been so sweet and understanding and I've treated you badly."

Kerri laughed and glanced down at her wrist-watch. "Let's forget it, shall we? Put it down to unrequited love or something. Come on, it's nearly lunchtime and after that long walk I'm starving."

They were just crossing the last stretch of sand, towards the small gate that led into the garden, when they heard raised voices, Dominic's and someone else's. As they drew nearer, they noticed the small red Volkswagen parked near the front door, and were just in time to see the two figures confronting each other. Kerri began to hustle Jane inside quickly as the girl showed every sign of joining them.

"Come on, Jane . . ."

Wildly, the girl shook her head.

"No — no . . . can't you *see* how angry Dominic is? He's got a violent temper, he's going to do something terrible to Mark . . ."

Glancing back at the tall young man, a good head taller than Dominic, deeply tanned by the sun and sea, at the bulging muscles beneath the white T-shirt with its university slogan, Kerri smiled. "I don't think so, Jane. Why don't we go indoors and change and see what Dominic has to say after they've talked it over?"

But it didn't turn out quite as he had anticipated. Kerri had just returned from her bedroom after changing into a dress, halter-necked with bold abstract flowers on a white background, when the front door swung open and the massive bulk of the blond youth came in, momentarily blocking out the light. And then, as he came farther into the hallway, she saw that he was carrying something in his arms, and that something happened to be a completely inert Dominic Prentice.

Kerri just stared at him stupidly for several long seconds, then hurried forward. She thanked her stars that Jane was still in her room.

"Bring him to the lounge," she said quickly. "We can lay him there."

The boy followed her along the passageway and passed through the door that she quickly held open. The young man strode into the large room, scarcely showing any outward signs of Dominic's weight, and lowered him to the settee. Straightening up, he looked at Kerri as she said, urgently, "What happened?"

"A slight difference of opinion between us, I'm afraid," said the boy slowly. "I'm really sorry that it had to come to this, but he's not hurt badly. He should be round in a minute or two."

As if to confirm his words, there was a low moan from the settee, and Dominic moved slightly.

"Should we send for a doctor?" Kerri asked.

Her knowledge of first aid was limited to sticking plasters and calamine lotion if she or any of her family stayed too long in the sun.

"I don't think that's necessary," replied the youth, bending over Dominic and investigating a small gash on his temple that was bleeding slightly. "It probably looks a lot worse than it is."

He smiled as he turned his head to look at her, then straightened to his full height, which was considerable. "I suppose I ought to introduce myself," he went on, still smiling. "Mark Kennedy, a friend of Jane's."

Kerri nodded. "I know. She told me about you. I'm Kerri Matheson, Jane's companion for the summer."

He nodded this time. "Yes, she told me about *you*."

Kerri's lips twisted. "I bet!" Her eyes went back to the now stirring figure on the settee. "Did you do that?" Her voice held awe.

She had not thought anyone capable of getting the better of Dominic.

"Not exactly." He shrugged, and turned to gaze down at the man. "We were having a few words — believe me, Miss Matheson, I had no intention of quarrelling with Jane's uncle, I had only come to try to explain things — about yesterday, you know — but before I could begin he flew off the handle and took a swing at me. I don't imagine he's had much practice at that sort of thing, for it was a pretty wild blow, and all I had to do was duck. Anyway, the next thing I knew his foot slipped on the wet gravel and he fell against the bonnet of the car." He gazed down at her. "The rear-view mirror I have on the door caught him on the forehead, and the next thing I knew he was out cold." And Kerri was glad to see that he had the grace to look sheepish.

At that moment Jane came into the room. The silence was almost electric as the two young people stood looking at each other and Kerri saw the vividly crimson blush that mounted the girl's cheeks before her gaze fell to her uncle.

"Kerri!" Her voice shook as she came forward. "What happened?"

Before Kerri could answer, the youth gave a slight cough, saying, "Look, Jane, why don't we go outside and I'll explain everything."

Without a word, Jane slipped her hand into his and they made for the door. Before they reached it, Kerri felt she had to have her say.

"Mark Kennedy, you're a coward," she said, severely. "Why don't you just admit that you don't want to be here when Mr Prentice comes round?"

"I don't want to be here when Mr Prentice comes round," he said, simply, then smiled as Jane cut in, feelingly, "Neither do I! You can handle this, Kerri, I'm pretty sure of that."

"I must say you have far more confidence in my abilities than I have myself," Kerri murmured, but the girl looked so appealing that she had to smile. A smile that widened as the two young people hurriedly disappeared through the open door as a small flutter of movement on the settee announced the imminent return of Dominic to consciousness.

Kerri dropped to her knees beside him and waited anxiously for his eyes to flicker open. Very soon they did, very briefly, then closed again.

"Come on," she said, softly. "You can do better than that. I'm surprised at you, a big strong man like you, acting like a Victorian miss."

He gingerly opened his eyes and looked up at her with a dazed expression. "Fat lot of sympathy I can expect from you, I can see," he muttered, none too clearly.

"It's your own fault entirely," she said. "You and your inflexible attitude in not allowing Jane to go anywhere or meet people of her own age. How do you feel?"

"Exceedingly bad," he said. "But no doubt if you hang round long enough it'll pass off."

Very carefully he propped himself up on one elbow and very gradually the paleness under his tan took on a bit of colour. With delicate fingers, he gently examined the cut on his head, and then stared with apparent horror at the slight smear of blood it left on his hand.

"Stay there," Kerri said, rising to her feet. "Don't go away. I'll be right back."

He looked vastly amused. "My dear girl, I have no intention of going anywhere, so your caution is quite unnecessary. I doubt whether I could if I tried."

She was just coming out of the bathroom with lint and hot water, when there was a patter of footsteps and Jane reappeared, her face troubled.

"Oh, Kerri, is my uncle all right? Mark told me how it happened. I suppose it's really my fault. If I hadn't met Mark like that, yesterday, it wouldn't have happened."

"We all know perfectly well that it *is* your fault, Jane," Kerri told her in a matter-of-fact voice. "But recriminations are going to help no one just now. Your uncle will probably want to talk about it later, but for the time being it can wait."

The girl hesitated and Kerri could see the struggle that was going on inside her. Rather more gently, Kerri added, "Wouldn't you like to help me see to his cut? It doesn't appear to be too bad, but we'll see what he says about sending for the doctor."

One hand flew to the girl's mouth. "A doctor? Oh, Kerri, is it *that* bad?"

"I don't think so, but we'd better see what he thinks."

"I don't see how I can possibly survive," said Dominic, in answer to her question when they returned to the lounge. "In such an event, your young man could well be had up for manslaughter."

Jane gasped and went white and

Kerri, feeling sorry for the girl, said disapprovingly, "Of course you know your uncle is teasing," and saw the almost imperceptible smile that came and went in Dominic's eye as he looked at her.

Jane blushed, then turned to ask politely, "If there's nothing I can do, Kerri, I think I'd rather go to my room."

Dominic nodded, and immediately regretted the movement. In a second Jane had gone and Kerri turned to the man on the settee. "I'm going to have a look at your cut," she told him, "so just lie still and try not to yell."

She bent down beside him and dabbed inexpertly at the afflicted place, and soon it was looking clean and not nearly as bad as it first appeared.

She left him for a moment and found a hand mirror, returning to show him the cut. "Do you think you need a doctor?" she asked, worriedly. "I don't know very much about such things . . . "

"No, of course not," he said. "I'm fine," and stood up.

Kerri rose with him and the next moment she was supporting his full weight on her shoulder as he wavered and almost collapsed. Hurriedly, he sat down again, lying back on the cushions with a wry grin.

"Well, maybe I'll just stay here a few minutes longer," he told her. "But a doctor, definitely, no."

He lifted his head and stared at her. "What happened to the blond giant? Don't tell me he actually *hit* me?"

Kerri shook her head. "No, Dominic, you fell, it seems, against the car. It must have been quite a fall. After bringing you in here, he explained to me what had happened and apologised. Then Jane appeared and they went outside to talk." Her lips twitched. "He admitted that he wasn't particularly keen on being here when you came to."

"Humph!" There was a short silence, then he said, "Anyway, I'll want to have a talk with that young man in the future. The very *near* future."

Kerri stared at him, at the hard lines that suddenly made his lips thin, outlined with white. "Why?" she demanded. "Why make it any worse? Jane's upset enough and I'm sure he feels just as badly, and he *did* admit that you took a swing at him first . . . ''

"You must be joking! He takes Jane off like that, knocks me cold, in spite of what he told you to the contrary, and you ask me to forget it!"

"You really are impossible at times," she retorted, unable to stop herself. "You keep Jane on a leash, barely letting her out of your sight, and hiring me to keep an eye on her when you're not around, and then the one time she *does* manage to meet people her own age and have some fun, you act like a Victorian father. *And* he didn't knock you cold. I told you, you fell."

His eyes were very dark as he looked at her. "Don't tell me you're enamoured with his charms, too?" he drawled.

She made an impatient gesture. "Oh, for heaven's sake . . . !" and he continued, equably, "Well, you did say I was impossible at times."

"Maybe impossible is too tame a word," she told him. "Maybe it doesn't register any more just *how* impossible you really are. Lots of people must have told you that, plenty of times before."

"No," he said, his face perfectly straight. "Most people seem afraid to say boo to me in case I turn around and jump on them."

"And do you?"

"Nearly always."

This time she couldn't help the smile from touching her mouth.

"*You* may think you're a pretty tough customer," she said, "but I think you ought to know that you don't scare me one bit, and that I refuse to be browbeaten like you do Jane."

"I was afraid of that," he said, and then grinned. "Do I really? Browbeat Jane, I mean?"

Then, as she turned to go, knowing he wasn't really expecting an answer, "Kerri!"

"Yes?"

"Don't you think the least you could do is assist a man injured in the course of young love to his room? I'll never make it on my own."

"I'll call Morello," she told him, solemnly, and closed the door behind her before he could think of some sarcastic comeback.

13

OVER breakfast the following morning Jane didn't appear. Kerri hurried over her meal then went back to her room to change. She had decided she would spend the morning on the beach and left word with one of the maids should Jane wish to join her. She dropped her towel on the sand and kicked off her pretty straw sandals.

The utter peace of the deserted beach soothed the indignant mood in which she had awakened. Now, motionless on the sand, Kerri felt as if she was poised on the edge of the world. She stretched languidly, enjoying the feeling of the sun on her skin, then jumped as a deep voice, behind her, said, "Good morning, Kerri. Am I interrupting something?"

Kerri forced herself not to react revealingly to that sardonic tone. Adopting a defiant expression, she turned and said, "Good morning, Dominic. No, you're not interrupting anything. I was just enjoying being alone." Her eyes travelled up to the white patch of sticking plaster on his forehead. "How are you feeling?"

"I'm all right," he said briefly. "I came to apologise. I behaved badly yesterday, and I'm sorry. There was a lot of truth in what you said about my attitude to Jane and her friends. I think I'm only now beginning to realise it."

Kerri almost gasped. She had expected many things — anger, rudeness, impatience, especially after the way she had spoken to him yesterday — but not this. Not him apologising to her. She almost wished he hadn't. She didn't want him to. It was much easier to deal with him when he remained his usual self — aloof and impassive.

"I — I — it's not necessary," she exclaimed ungraciously.

"I disagree." There was only a few feet between them now and his nearness was too disconcerting. "My only excuse was that — well, I was worried about Jane. You must have known that. Even so, I had no right to act like I did. In spite of your opinion of me, I'm not always so ill-mannered."

Kerri drew the short towelling jacket about her, holding the collar close at the throat with one hand. She was supremely conscious of his nearness and she half thought he knew it and was taking great delight in it.

"Well, I suppose Jane did do wrong to stay away so long. Especially without telling anyone where she had gone."

"Yes, she could at least have done that."

He was leaning towards her, supporting himself on one hand and Kerri's eyes were riveted to the fine dark hairs that covered the back of his arm.

"Anyway," he went on, "it isn't serious, as we at first thought, and maybe in future Jane will think of informing me of her intentions before she goes out."

Kerri grimaced. She forced herself to meet his eyes. "And if she should ask you first, would you let her go?"

He shrugged. "It would depend on where she was going, wouldn't it, and with whom. You must know by now, Kerri, just what an unpredictable man you're working for."

During the following few days Jane was in her old prickly mood and spent most of the time watching the driveway for the reappearance of the little red volkswagen. Privately, Kerri thought it would be expecting a lot of the blond youth to return after what had happened. She walked with Jane on the beach, swam and sunbathed, but, try as she might, she could draw no more than the briefest responses from the girl or even make a small dent in the barriers she had erected around herself. Unable to approach her on any level, in the end Kerri concentrated solely on the aspect that she knew was uppermost on Dominic's mind, and she, too, watched carefully for the young man and his car.

Sunday dawned, with dark clouds over the horizon, a warning of further unseasonable weather, and the atmosphere in the house matched the weather exactly. Kerri had managed to avoid seeing Dominic all day, which was a relief, but, as if to make up for it, Jane decided to be twice as difficult as usual.

She had apparently decided she did not want Kerri's company at all that day and, with an ease that made Kerri wince, she managed to give her the slip several times, only reappearing when it suited her or when she thought she had worried Kerri enough.

It was a game to her, and one at which she was very adept.

By evening, Kerri was irritable and bad-tempered, something that seldom happened to her before she had come to this place. It struck her that the girl who would leave would not be quite the same person who had walked so blithely on to that plane in England.

Jane, like her uncle, was an enigma.

Almost ashamed of the wonderful time she was having on the island, Kerri was seized with a desire to give her attention wholeheartedly to her young charge, whether Jane welcomed it or not. Over breakfast that morning Dominic had told them that he would have to leave for the mainland later that day and would be gone for a few days. He didn't say so, but Kerri knew that he was going to wind up his business affairs there with the museum. She clung to every moment that he had with them in the later summer sunshine on the terrace, knowing that when he returned they would be packing their bags for home.

She set to with keeping Jane occupied, with renewed vigour. She knew that the last few days had been nothing but a series of disappointments for the younger girl, for the days went by and still there was no sign, or word, of the blond Mark.

Often during the day, when they were resting after swimming, or walking, she noticed Jane's eyes, wandering garden-wards, hoping against hope that the young man would appear.

She tried to make herself as entertaining as possible, hoping that the girl would soon forget him. But she knew this was expecting a lot. First love, calf love, call it what you will, was too precious to forget so easily. Jane would remember for a long time yet that large, blond young man who had lured her away for one fun-filled evening . . .

In the evenings, sitting in Jane's room, telling Jane about some of the more ridiculous events of her childhood with her brother, she would notice the brooding look come into Jane's brown eyes and search her memories for something to keep her amused. Lying on the bed, her chin on her propped up hands, Jane listened half-heartedly to Kerri's reminiscences. When the subject had been exhausted, Kerri wondered what else they could talk about, for really, apart from being young, the two girls had little in common. Jane turned on her back, gazing at Kerri with pursed lips.

"What does your father do?"

"He works in an insurance office. He's been in the same job ever since my mother and he were married."

"And have you lived in the same house, too?"

Kerri nodded. "We have. Both my brother and I were born there."

"Doesn't it get awfully boring? I think I should hate living in the same place from one year's end to another."

"No, why should it? It's a very secure feeling, knowing that nothing will ever change."

Jane gazed at her pensively. "But how can you be so sure of that? That nothing will ever change?"

"I can't, of course. It's just that one hopes that nothing will ever change, if you've had a happy childhood as we had, my brother and I. Our home was the centre of our world, the night inside always with the same bright places, the same dark places, everything pleasant and in order, safe from all the horrible outside things because my father and mother were always there. It was the way my parents had made it, sustained by their love and goodness. It fitted me — *fits* me well enough. It would hurt too much to give it up now."

Why had she changed the tense, she wondered. Didn't her home still fit her? Wouldn't she always be living there, at least until, in the far distant future, she met some man and married . . .

She pushed the thought, unbidden and positively unwelcome, away, and looking up met Jane's eyes. They were bright, full of what looked like anger, and Kerri was immediately penitent. "Jane! If I've said anything to upset you I'm sorry . . . "

Jane shook her head, looking away. "It's just the way you talk about your mother . . . " She rose from the bed, abruptly, and went to brush her hair in front of the mirror. "I'm sorry," said Kerri again. "It was thoughtless of me."

For a few moments there was silence in the room, then Kerri, wanting to know, yet wondering if she was being wise, said, "Jane, don't think I'm prying, but what happened to *your* mother? I know she died, but . . . "

Jane turned to face her, eyes huge and blank, full of reproach in the white face. "She drowned. My father and her and Dominic were sailing off the coast of Greece and the boat capsized. Dominic saved my father, but my mother drowned." She spoke with such bitterness that Kerri flinched.

Kerri stared at her in horror. "Oh, no! Jane, I'm sorry! I would never have asked if I'd known . . . "

"How *were* you to know unless someone told you?" The two girls stared at each other, then Jane said, "He let my mother drown, you know. He could have saved her but he chose instead to save my father."

"I'm sure you're wrong, Jane. Dominic would never deliberately have . . . "

"That's why he's always so diligent about offering to have me for the summers. His conscience bothers him."

★ ★ ★

Kerri spent the next few days aching to see Dominic come driving back along the flower-lined driveway, yet dreading it at the same moment because it would mean the end of the summer spent on Lessane. Also, after Jane's disturbing disclosure, she knew she would view him now in a different light.

She was still shattered by what Jane had told her about her mother's death, shattered, too, by the cool bitterness with which Jane discussed it. But she didn't waste too much time trying to fathom her attitude. After living with the girl for most of the summer she was familiar by now with her odd changes of temperament.

But there was a line of thought which caused her considerable worry once she had gone to bed and the house was silent.

Had Dominic really left the woman to

drown, even unintentionally? Had that been the reason for his unexpected panic, almost instantly repressed, that day on the beach, when she'd thought Jane was in difficulties? Kerri knew now that his circumspection where Jane was concerned had its roots in that day of long ago when the girl's mother had met her fate.

How old had Jane been? she wondered. What sort of life could she expect with an uncle who considered himself the cause of her mother's death, and a father who just couldn't care where his daughter was, just as long as she wasn't troubling him? What bothered her more than anything else, they were now approaching the end of summer. Some of the boarding-schools opened early, if not to start work, to accept early boarders who had nowhere else to go. It was a cert that after the episode with the blond guy, Dominic, having had as much as he could stand of his niece's contrary behaviour, would pack her off back to school. And, if he did, he would have no use for Kerri, either.

The thought made her heart beat in a particularly hollow way. She couldn't face the thought of returning to England just yet, or that Jane would be thrust back into that sterile atmosphere she hated.

There would be no more bright, sun-filled mornings, no more breakfast on the terrace, with the sounds of the ocean all about them, the taste of salt fresh on her lips, dark velvet nights when the moon made an amber pathway over the slumbering island. But bleakest of all, no Dominic . . .

To her relief, Dominic, when he returned to Lessane, made no more mention of sending his niece back to school, or indeed, of leaving the island. Kerri gathered by the odd remark he made that his work on the manuscript was finished and now he felt he was able to relax and enjoy himself before returning to the bleakness of an English winter.

They spent most of their time on the beach. For Kerri they were idyllic days. He drove them to the hotel and charmed them on to the tennis courts. Kerri, who hadn't played tennis since she'd left school, was particularly inept. But Jane was quite good, and Kerri was

243

persuaded, and the hotel coach, who was working out his last few weeks of the summer contract, obliged them by making a fourth.

They visited Maili and the bazaar, this time Kerri buying presents to take back to her family, and a length of misty blue and lilac Indian cotton she thought her mother might like for a semi-evening dress. They sat with tall drinks at the beach café, watching the tourists, and Kerri felt a pang of sadness for the young girl when she noticed how eagerly she watched for the blond head towering above the rest of the crowd.

But it seemed that Mark Kennedy was no longer on the island, or if he was, he was no longer interested in Jane.

Jane's eyes had a particular brilliance about them as they searched the crowd, knowing it was fruitless. The girl was very quiet, as, indeed, she had been for days, so that Kerri could not help wondering if she had had another session with her uncle, or just another bad night and, possibly, nightmare. She sat hunched together, gazing broodingly across the stretch of water before them as though it didn't exist, once her eyes had given up the fruitless task of watching for the tall bond youth.

But Kerri had to admit that she wasn't wholly with the younger girl these days. Her entire being was centered on Dominic. With all this outdoor life and sunshine, he had developed an attractive tan, and his face, prone to dourness through too much concentration on his work, or so Kerri suspected, had become mellowed into more relaxed, handsome lines.

In the evenings, tremendous in his dinner jacket, the sight of him was enough to make Kerri's whole being melt like a candle in the sun.

In the warm, flower-scented evenings, he didn't wait to ask the girls if they would like to walk on the beach. Casually, he would take each girl by the arm, walking between them, guiding them along the edge of the water, often laughing as they skipped back to avoid a sudden tempestuous wave. Once, when Jane's silver sandals became soaked through by her not moving back in time, he advised her to go in and change.

"Seawater won't do those flimsy things a lot of good," he told her.

Jane nodded and did as she was bid.

Gazing after the small figure, Kerri murmured, "Young love can be so painful when it's not reciprocated."

She saw his frown. "Who said it wasn't reciprocated?"

"Well, that boy hasn't once tried to see her since that night, hasn't even phoned to find out how you were . . . "

"He did. He phoned a number of times during that week. I took all the calls in my study."

"Then why . . . ?" Kerri looked puzzled and he gave a short laugh, again taking her arm and urging her along the stretch of smooth sand. "Look, Kerri, my niece is a young, impressionable girl. There will be a lot of boys like that before she meets the right one. Let's not make a big thing about it, eh?"

"I — I think you're being unreasonable," she exclaimed, her lips trembling. "You're — you're positively sanctimonious in your attitude towards Jane. You've permitted the position you hold and your conscience to distort your view . . . "

His eyes narrowed, as hard as the wintry skies they resembled. "Yes, I have," he agreed harshly. "And you had better remember it. Now sheathe your claws or you will shock Jane. Here she is now."

It would have been more dignified to have refused to complete that moonlight walk by the sleeping ocean, but the sight of the smile on his face, teasing, provoking, caused her to walk on in silence, trying to still the jumble of sensations that that particular smile always brought.

However, the very next morning her spirits had risen mercurially and she joined Jane at breakfast on the terrace. There was the silver coffee-pot and the tall jug of fruit juice, from which Jane was helping herself. There was grilled bacon and eggs, and freshly baked rolls with chilled curls of butter.

"I'm starving," she exclaimed, sitting down and shaking the white linen table napkin across her lap. Jane gave her a ded smile. "You always are starving. I can't think how you manage to keep so slim with your appetite."

Kerri laughed and took a mouthful of the fresh chilled orange juice.

"What are we going to do today?" she asked, gazing at the girl over the rim of her glass. "Don't you feel like doing something different? Maybe Dominic, if he's in a good mood, will take us out in the car."

"My uncle left early this morning," Jane told her. "I heard him drive off before I was up."

Kerri pulled a face. "Oh, well, never mind . . . " She tried to still the feeling of disappointment that the girl's words brought. How long would he be away this time? she wondered . . .

She had no time to think about this further, for just then there was the sound of a car engine in the driveway and Jane lifted her head, like a hunting-dog listening for his master's voice in a grouse-shoot. There were low voices in the lounge behind them, Dominic and someone else's, and Jane's eyes widened unbelievingly. Kerri followed her gaze and was startled to see a tall thin man with Dominic.

She had so expected the newcomer to be Mark Kennedy that she was even more flabbergasted when she saw Jane jump to her feet and cry, "Daddy!"

14

THE girl flung her table napkin to the floor and ran to the tall man, arms outstretched. "Oh, Daddy, is it really you? I can't believe it . . . "

The dark-haired, lean-faced man came forward, and gathered Jane into a bearlike hug. Then laughter, stuttered incoherence from Jane, started and Kerri felt Dominic's arm about her waist, guiding her towards the low gate that opened on to the beach. "I don't think we're needed any more."

Kerri allowed him to lead her across the beach until they came to the deep shade of a cluster of palms. Kerri looked up at him with a dazed smile.

"Was that really Jane's father?"

Dominic nodded. "I got in touch with my brother soon after the police brought Jane back that evening." He gave Kerri his flinty gleam. "I explained to him just how Jane was being affected by his — perhaps quite unintentional, indifference, and that, as a father, I thought it was about time he showed some concern for his daughter. I think I made him see my point of view."

"And he flew over straight away?"

Dominic nodded again. "He flew over straight away. Early this morning I received a telephone call from the airport to say he had arrived and drove over to fetch him."

"And that, really, is all that Jane wants." Kerri sighed happily, turning towards the house to see Jane and her father sitting close together, the girl's face more animated than Kerri had seen it for a long time, talking as though speech was going out of fashion.

Dominic's lips twitched. "Well, perhaps, not all . . . "

Kerri looked at him, and nodded, glad that his voice sounded less hard, more assenting than she had ever heard it. "Yes, perhaps not all, but maybe she will get the chance to see *him* again, if he's still on the island."

Dominic smiled down into her eyes. "Little Miss Matchmaker herself! What about you, Kerri? Isn't there someone, on the island or at home, that you're dying to see again?"

Kerri shook her head. The catch on her wrist-watch suddenly needed all her attention. How could she allow him to see what was in her eyes, perhaps recognise the aching longing there . . . ? "No, not really. No one in particular, that is."

"I'm disappointed to hear it. I should have thought a girl with your looks would have had dozens of boys, buzzing about you like bees about a honeypot."

Again she shook her head. "Then you would be wrong, wouldn't you?"

Dominic slanted her a jaded smile and said with feeling, "What we both need is a drink. Come on."

As he guided her back to the house, choosing the side entrance instead of the one leading to the terrace, Kerri said, slightly shocked, "It's barely breakfast-time! You can't have a drink at this time of the morning!"

"Don't quibble. You can have a drink at any time of the morning, as far as I'm concerned."

But when they sat in the study that

held such memories, he instructed the maid to bring her coffee while he poured himself a brandy. As they sat soaking up the peace in that quiet room, Kerri began to feel the reaction of more than a week of tension. A heavy lethargy overtook her. Her eyelids felt heavy with the warmth of the sunlight coming through the large window.

From miles away she heard Dominic say, "All that remains now is for us to pack, and we can be on our way. Do you think you could be ready by tomorrow, Kerri?"

Somehow she managed, calmly enough, "Yes, Dominic, easily."

He nodded. "Good. Then I'll get on the phone and book us seats on tomorrow's flight."

Jane was like an incoherent child, wildly excited at the prospect of living with her father, for he had admitted to Dominic that it was time he took an interest in his daughter, and from now on she would live with him.

"And I don't have to go back to that awful school?" Jane demanded.

Her father gazed at her consideringly.

"Well, of course, you'll have to finish your education, Jane. But we can talk about that later." Meeting Kerri's curious gaze, he explained, "For the next few years I shall be stationed in Kenya, quite close to a town where there are, I believe, quite good schools. Jane will be able to go to one of them."

Jane gave her a knowing glance. "And, Kerri, guess what? Dominic, quite by chance, has found out a certain person's address, so I shall be able to write to him. Isn't it all just fabulous?"

Kerri didn't have to ask who the certain person was. The glowing expression on Jane's face told her all too clearly. She just prayed that the girl wouldn't be disappointed, that it would not prove to be a one-sided affair, with the feeling all on her side.

Dominic, meanwhile, had made all the plans for their immediate departure. Kerri had moved like an automaton as she packed, happy for Jane, downcast for her own immediate future. The sun-bronzed girl with the wide blue eyes that she occasionally caught glimpses of in the mirror, who should by all accounts be looking ecstatic at the prospect of seeing her family and home again, after so long, seemed to have no connection with herself.

Heathrow was its usually noisy self, travellers searching frantically for mislaid luggage, listening against the background of noise for the announcement that would tell them that their journey was about to begin.

Kerri walked with Dominic through the crowded passageways and when finally he hurled their luggage from the rest of the moving suitcases, he turned to her and said, "How are you getting back to town? Won't you let me give you a lift?"

Kerri shook her head. She didn't want to be beholden to this man any more than she could help. "No, thank you, Dominic. I'll get the Underground into town and from there it's easy enough to get a train to High Linton." She smiled, "Or I just might telephone Neil to come for me."

He gazed at her thoughtfully, opened his mouth as though about to argue further, then seemed to decide otherwise. "As you wish."

There was a sound of a voice calling his name and he turned, the smile on his lips widening when he saw Nicole Dalny. She was wearing a white wool suit with a jacket bedecked with an enormous fluffy tan fur collar. She ran forward, her voice high and clear above the babble of the crowd. "Dominic, what luck! I wasn't too sure when you'd be arriving, but how glad I am that I came . . . "

He greeted her with a swift kiss dropped on top of the glossy dark head. "Nicole . . . !"

Kerri bent and picked up her bags and walked away, pushing her way through the hurrying throng. She was home before she knew it. The day promised to be one of mild sunshine, in spite of the fact that it was early November. Kerri woke late. Prolonged silence told her that her father and Neil had already left for work and that her mother had caught the bus to do her weekly shopping.

The house seemed empty and dull, the smell of life was all outside, a faint whiff like soil turned cold-side-up to the sun. She called her friend, Janice, who had delighted her husband by producing the desired son and heir, and arranged to meet for lunch.

The restaurant was counterfeit gypsy-style, with red plush benches and peasant pottery, although there was a very English air about its patrons, elderly ladies in winter coats and hats, meeting for a lunch and gossip session in town.

Her friend was wearing a new coat and soft leather boots that ended just below the knee. She looked well and the fat baby, wrapped securely in its knitted shawl with mittens on the tiny waving fists, smiled up at her from the new and expensive pram and gurgled.

"Tom is so pleased it was a boy," she exclaimed, regarding the child as though he was the most beautiful creature in the world, as indeed he was, as any mother would think, gazing at her first-born. "Of course, I was glad to hear from you, Kerri," she went on, bending to tuck the shawl more securely under the baby's chin, "but it isn't easy, getting away at this time of the day. Thank goodness that he's a fairly good baby and sleeps a lot."

Kerri murmured protestingly that she

should have said so at once, and they could have arranged to meet another time. The young mother smiled. "Oh, well, mustn't grumble. Believe me, Kerri, this infant takes almost every minute of my spare time when he's awake. I can see I'll easily become a cabbage if I don't make the effort."

The room hummed around them, the waiters busy serving lunches. Later Janice patted her hair and felt for her gloves. "I admit it's exhausting, having a baby, Kerri, but I wouldn't be without him now for the world. Didn't you . . . ?"

She pursed her lips, gazing at Kerri consideringly. "Didn't you, on that fabulous island, meet someone special? I'm sure there must have been plenty of chances."

Kerri smiled thinly. With Dominic there, she hadn't wanted to meet anyone else. She shook her head. "No, not a soul."

Janice looked puzzled. "But there must have been lots of guys. In a place like that . . . "

"No." Kerri's voice was quite firm. "I didn't meet a single person in whom I could feel interested."

Janice got up vigorously. "I've got to get my bus. Thanks, Kerri. The idea of lunch was a good one. Maybe we can do it every so often? It'll be my treat next time remember."

"That would be nice. We'll arrange something soon."

Outside, the sham summer day, gilded with sunshine, was overlaid with the chill of approaching winter. Kerri got off the bus and, suddenly cold, she folded her arms to hug her own warmth and crossed the bridge. She leaned on the parapet and looked down at the water, golden and copper, reflecting the weak sunlight.

Her mother was waiting as she opened the small gate and walked up the narrow pathway. "Kerri! For heaven's sake, where have you been?"

"I met Janice for lunch," she explained, wondering why her mother should sound so distracted. "Then I just missed the early bus and had to wait for the later one."

Her mother waved her explanations away with an impatient hand. "There is someone waiting to see you. I must say he's been very patient. He's been waiting for ages."

Kerri stared, and pushed open the front door and entered the hall behind her mother. Trying to still her suddenly trembling hands, she removed her coat and hung it neatly on the old-fashioned hallstand. "Oh, really? Who?"

Mrs Matheson smiled and pushed open the door of the front room. "You'll see," was her cryptic answer.

The over-grown Virginia creeper outside the window, something her father had almost meant to prune but never did, made the room dim and for a moment Kerri stood and gazed about her, thinking whoever had been waiting had got tired and left. "Hello, Kerri!"

She tried to speak but words would not come, then she turned, her eyes blinded by the rush of foolish tears. Then he was beside her, his hand closing over hers still on the door handle and removing it as she made to pull open the door and leave. "What, going already?"

His voice held the usual scorn, making her flush deepen.

She turned to face him, defiantly, small

chin lifting in a gesture that made his eyes soften. "Why are you here?"

"I wanted to see you. After you left, so hurriedly at the airport, I felt we hadn't said our goodbyes properly. I drove over with the intention of bearding you in your den, only you were out and your mother wasn't sure when you'd be back. She said I was welcome to wait, though. I must say she makes a wonderful cup of tea, and her home-made scones are out of this world."

Kerri made an impatient gesture. "Let's talk about why you're here, shall we, Dominic, and leave out my mother's home-made scones."

"Very well," he grinned. "Although, I must say, they will take some leaving."

She felt the old weakness, the trembling, coming back at his nearness. She walked away, toward the window, gazing out over the winter-seared garden, the drift of fallen leaves under the ancient oak on the lawn. Finally, when the silence threatened to go on for ever, she turned to face him, her features taut and cold. "Well?"

"Well, what?" Infuriatingly, he stared

back at her, not the merest flicker of expression on his to show his feelings.

"Why have you come to see me? I thought our business was finished when Jane went back with her father. Unless you — are offering me another job."

His lips pursed thoughtfully. "It's an idea, at that. *Would* you accept it if I did?"

"That would depend on what it was, wouldn't it?"

He came close to the window, close to her and put his hand under her chin, lifting her face and forcing her to meet his eyes in the old imperious way. "Why did you run away from me, Kerri, that day at the airport? Towards our last few days on the island I rather thought we had become friends. Was your friendship too much to ask for? If so, you should have had the sagacity to tell me, sweet Kerri, and not run away."

He paused for a moment, but she said nothing, so he continued, "Perhaps now it is time I *demanded* the answers to a few questions. Don't you agree?"

She looked up at the arrogant lines of the face that had tormented her dreams, waking and sleeping, for so long, and she blinked rapidly, trying in vain to stop the flow of tears before they started, as she slowly shook her head.

"I — see." His breath escaped in a long sigh, as if he had been holding it for her answer. "Anyway, I'm going to ask, whether you answer or not is your business. My first question is: how *do* you feel about coming back to work for me? The second is, it wouldn't be on the island, but here in England, probably at my home in Westleigh. There would be a lot of travelling attached to it, but I shouldn't think you'd mind that."

"And what would you require me to do?" she ground out. "Keep Mrs Dalny company while you're away?"

It was out now, that which had been bothering her, and she didn't know whether to be glad or sorry.

"Nicole?" He looked puzzled as she said, wretchedly, "I didn't mean it to sound like that. I'm sorry."

"What exactly do you mean, then?"

"Nicole Dalny." Her voice faltered almost to a whisper and he had to bend his head to catch the low words.

"She's your mistress, isn't she? Are you going to marry her now and make it legal? If you are, I don't see why you need me . . . !"

When she looked up again his face was bleak. "I've never pretended to anyone that I'm a saint, Kerri. I admit Nicole and I had a thing going at one time, and very sweet it was, too, but that was over long ago. Mrs Dalny helps me with my work. Perhaps you didn't know, but she's an extremely accomplished artist and is doing the illustrations for the new book I've just finished. We're going over it once more before it is sent to the publishers."

She caught her breath, feeling everything falling into place. "I'm sorry, I didn't know . . . "

He smiled brightly. "This isn't going to make sense to you, but, when I was a little boy, my father used to tell James and me — 'Don't waste precious time searching for the gold when you can have the rainbow'."

"The rainbow being . . . ?"

"A happy home life, a wife who loves me and, what is more important, can put up with my disposition, which, as you will be the first to agree, is anything but consistent." His voice gentled. "Nicole is like the gold, hard and implacable, very nice to have but something that can be easily lost. Give me the rainbow every time."

His gaze made her suddenly shy and she stared at the carpet, tracing the faded green pattern of ivy leaves with one toe.

A picture came to her — Jane, standing before the mirror, hairbrush in hand, her face strained and white as she said, "He let my mother drown, you know. He could have saved her but he chose in stead to save my father."

Looking up she saw he was regarding her with a touch of irritation.

"Well," he said, "you haven't answered my question. Do you want to come back to me or not?"

She met his eyes head on. "I want to hear in your own words the truth about Jane's mother," she said, aghast at her own temerity. "She told me that you'd — you'd let her mother drown . . . I just couldn't . . ."

"Couldn't believe that what Jane said

was true? I was wondering when Jane would bring up that subject. It was. Every word of it. I let Emma drown."

She gave a little cry, but he wasn't listening. "You see, I knew my brother couldn't swim. I also knew that Emma was a strong swimmer, that she would be able to cling on to the upturned boat until I got my brother to safety. Unfortunately, it didn't quite work out like that. When I got back, having seen James safely ashore, Emma was nowhere to be seen. I think I dived and redived until I was exhausted, until someone came and forced me to give up."

"But it wasn't your fault . . . "

He shook his head. "It was my fault. I should have known she couldn't have held on in that sea. Not long enough for me to have come back for her."

"And yet, if you'd saved her, your brother would have . . . "

She stared at him and he gave a grim nod. "Exactly. Life is perplexing. One never knows what to do for the best — until it is too late. Perhaps you understand now why I am so fiercely protective of Jane. She was only a baby when she lost her mother. Having her with me as much as possible I feel in some way I'm atoning for my past sins."

Kerri stared at him, shocked speechless by his confession, by the grim pain that showed on his face. Adding to the feeling of shock, he went on, relentlessly, as though driving himself to say everything that had to be said, once and for all, "Especially as at one time Emma and I had been lovers."

Kerri bent her head wretchedly, unable any longer to look into those eyes. "I was young," he said, "not yet twenty. Emma was beautiful and glamorous, a woman of the world. I loved her passionately from the first moment I saw her. She was engaged to my brother, who is six years older than me, but she soon let me know that she preferred me. Oh, I'm not making excuses. I wanted her. I was as crazy about her as she seemed about me. It got rather out of hand, our affair, and with James being away so much, well, it didn't help. I never meant it to happen, and I'm sure she didn't either. I would never have believed myself capable of so strong a . . . "

His voice shook and Kerri felt something tighten inside her, like a spring ready to snap. It hurt. It hurt so much that she held herself tense, waiting for it to snap. Dominic was speaking again, " . . . so strong an infatuation. That's what it was. After a time I saw that. For a little while we had both lost our heads and . . . "

He paused again, hearing after all those years the shrill angry voice of the woman when he'd tried to tell her. "You've got it all worked out, haven't you? All so tidy and civilised. It was just a pleasant little episode that is now closed, neatly tied up ready to be put away. But not for me." Her face came back vividly to his mind, and he wondered, comparing the pale, flower-like beauty of the girl standing so tensely before him, why he had ever thought her beautiful. "Didn't it occur to you that I might feel different?" Emma had screamed. "Didn't it matter that I believed you when you said you loved me?"

"Please, Emma," he'd begged. "There are people along the beach. Do you want them to hear you?"

"I don't care *who* hears me. My God, what a fool I've been! You're just like your dear brother, all sweetness and light until one gets to know you, and then you're a vastly different proposition . . . "

"Emma!" There had been anguish in his voice. "It wasn't like that. I swear it. I thought I loved you. I *did* love you . . ."

"And now your conscience is worrying you, is that it? I happen to be engaged to your brother and that makes it a sacred bond, one that I'm unable to break. Come off it, Dominic. I can break my engagement to James just like that," she snapped her fingers, "and wouldn't give it a second thought. It's you I want, not your dear, industrious brother with the dust of ancient civilisations in his blood and archaeological finds for feelings."

He had shaken her roughly. "Emma! Talk sense. You don't know what you're saying. Have you the slightest idea what it would do to James if he found out that we . . . ?"

"Had had an affair?" One corner of her full mouth tilted. "Go on, why don't

269

you say it? I shall. I shall shout it from the rooftops, the whole, horrible, furtive affair."

"*Will you be quiet, Emma?* My dear, please try to calm down. Be sensible."

"Sensible? Why should I be? What have I got to lose *if* everyone knows about it?" The words broke from her in a harsh bray of laughter and before he could stop her she had turned and was running away . . .

"Barely a month later she married my brother," he murmured. "Then two summers later we went for that ill-omened cruise in the Aegean Sea, leaving Jane in the care of a nursemaid . . . Well, you know what happened. What made everything so much worse was, at the funeral, James told me, with tears in his eyes, "I was aware that Emma didn't love me, she always seemed so preoccupied and never really took much interest in Jane, right from the start, but I didn't blame her. She was such a wonderful wife for any man to have, so lovely, that one forgave her her small transgressions." I don't know to this day if he ever had any idea about

Emma and me . . . " He turned away from her. "Oh, goddammit!"

The silence was ghastly. It was the silence of a human being appalled, when your heart tells you one thing and your reason another. Kerri's heart whispered, "He was only a boy, too gullible to withstand the charms of the beautiful Emma," while her reason argued different. He began to walk about the room, aimlessly, hands thrust in his pockets while she watched him, her whole being tense with pity. Her knees were uncontrollably shaking. After a while, when he'd stood looking out of the window for so long she'd become alarmed at his silence, he turned to face her, to say, "Well, now that you know the worst about me, what about my offer. *Will* you come back with me to Westleigh?"

"You don't need a housekeeper; you have a very able woman in the one I saw that day, *or* a companion for Jane. Perhaps a secretary . . . ?"

Dominic shook his head, and in the same tone of voice he would have asked her to dance, he said, "If you don't find me too despicable, how would you like to marry me?"

"Don't joke, Dominic. I hardly think marriage is the subject for fun." It was a painful effort to get it out.

"I'm not joking, Kerri. Believe me, I'm not joking. I don't think I've ever been more serious in my whole life. I've been such a fool . . . " Suddenly, before she was aware of his intentions, he drew her to him, his eyes searching her face with a curious intensity, then he bent, and his mouth was gentle and restrained on hers. "Think about it, sweet Kerri, about sharing the rest of our lives together, and in the morning I'll come and expect my answer."

He kissed her again and it was as if he was setting a seal on a vow that had already been made. As the door closed behind him Kerri sat down on the low settee, her knees shaking under her. In just a few minutes her entire world had turned on its head, she thought in bewilderment. She pressed her hands to her cheeks, hearing Dominic's deep voice, pleasant and genial, talking to her mother in the hallway, followed a few seconds later by the sound of a car being driven away. There was no question of joining her mother in the kitchen now, as she usually did about this time, preparing supper for her father and Neil. She was so shaken by what had just occurred — Dominic's proposal plus the terrible confession that must have caused him considerable pain to reveal — that she was hardly able to think coherently.

And yet — she was unable to ignore or subdue the sweet, warm elation which at Dominic's kiss had swept through her body, carrying any lingering doubts or misgivings away on a tide of certainty . . .

She closed her eyes, leaning back against the worn sofa, dizzy with happiness, and let her mind dwell on the cool dark arrogance of his face and the glow in the light grey eyes that gazed back at her.

She thought of his large, rather gloomy house at Westleigh, visualising the rooms filled with flowers, log fires glowing in the grates, driving out the gloominess.

She already knew what her answer would be. No need to wait until tomorrow. She rose and went to her father's study, to telephone.

The cold voice of the woman she had met, aeons ago, answered her call.

Mr Prentice was not yet home.

She left a message for him to call her, just as soon as he got back, and gave her number. The evening passed. She sat with her family after supper, watching a TV show. At least, her eyes watched, but as far as she was concerned the screen might have been blank. Dominic didn't call back. At ten o'clock she kissed her mother and said goodnight and went upstairs.

How could she be sure Dominic had meant what he said? Wasn't it just another aspect of the unconformity of the man? She had believed him and with a man like Dominic that would be fatal. Too many women had already fallen under his spell. She swallowed the sudden lump in her throat, and dashed away the tears that squeezed past her eyelids with the back of her hand.

Damn Dominic! Oh, damn him! Momentarily she had let herself be blinded by the glamorous summer on the island, blinded, most of all, by Dominic Prentice himself.

But she was home now, back with her own kind of people and never again would she allow herself to be deluded into thinking it was love when it was all merely a sham.

The gold and the rainbow! She thought back to his words. Not for a man like Dominic the will-o'-the-wisp colours of the rainbow. Rather the more substantial hard gold that bought the good things in life that he seemed to expect.

Even his sentiments about that had been a circumvention of the truth.

She fell asleep at last.

They were having breakfast the next morning when there was the sound of a car stopping outside the front gate. "What . . . ?" began her father and Mrs Matheson frowned. "Early for visitors," she remarked. Kerri's father rose and went into the hallway. There were voices, then her father came back, and behind him, towering in the doorway, Kerri could see Dominic Prentice.

Kerri caught her breath. Why bother to come now, when he hadn't even returned her call. Unless something happened to Jane . . .

"Sorry I interrupted your meal," Dominic said smoothly, smiling at her mother. "I'll wait outside by the car until you are finished."

But Mrs Matheson was shaking her head. "You'll do nothing of the sort, young man. Sit down. At least have a cup of tea with us."

"If you insist."

Acutely aware of him throughout the rest of the meal, Kerri kept her eyes lowered to her plate, and when at last it was over, her mother gave her a little push towards the front room. "Go and entertain your visitor, Kerri. I'll manage the washing-up."

Kerri felt Dominic's hand reach out for, and find, hers, holding it firmly as though warning her that there was no further chances of escape.

After the briefest hesitation, she gave in, and followed him into the comfortable sitting-room.

"Good luck," called Neil, maddeningly, after them, and the laughter in his voice chased away the sardonic lines in Dominic's face, making him look, suddenly, years younger.

"Thanks."

The door closed behind them with a dull thud and Dominic turned to face her.

"You've got a nerve," began Kerri, "coming here like this. Why didn't you answer my telephone call?"

He smiled at her benevolently. "I only got the message this morning — I don't think Mrs Hodge likes you, which might make for complications. Don't you agree?"

"No, I don't agree. If Mrs Hodge doesn't like me then she'll have to go."

"Are you mad? She's indispensable."

"What makes her indispensable?"

"She's a wonderful cook for one thing, and she's looked after me for years." He checked himself. "There we go, fighting again. When we're married, you know, this will have to stop."

They stared at each other, first in consternation and then with growing amusement. Then — "How did you know my answer wouldn't be 'no'?" demanded Kerri.

"Let's just say I'm psychic," he grinned.

"Let's just say you've got a colossal ego," she replied, mouth quirking.

He gazed behind them at the closed door. "I wonder if your mother will want to dust in here or anything?" he said, a trifle apprehensively.

"She's far too sensible — I hope," she replied, and went into his arms with a contented sigh.

THE END

Other titles in the
Ulverscroft Large Print Series:

TO FIGHT THE WILD
Rod Ansell and Rachel Percy

Lost in uncharted Australian bush, Rod Ansell survived by hunting and trapping wild animals, improvising shelter and using all the bushman's skills he knew.

COROMANDEL
Pat Barr

India in the 1830s is a hot, uncomfortable place, where the East India Company still rules. Amelia and her new husband find themselves caught up in the animosities which seethe between the old order and the new.

THE SMALL PARTY
Lillian Beckwith

A frightening journey to safety begins for Ruth and her small party as their island is caught up in the dangers of armed insurrection.

THE WILDERNESS WALK
Sheila Bishop

Stifling unpleasant memories of a misbegotten romance in Cleave with Lord Francis Aubrey, Lavinia goes on holiday there with her sister. The two women are thrust into a romantic intrigue involving none other than Lord Francis.

THE RELUCTANT GUEST
Rosalind Brett

Ann Calvert went to spend a month on a South African farm with Theo Borland and his sister. They both proved to be different from her first idea of them, and there was Storr Peterson — the most disturbing man she had ever met.

ONE ENCHANTED SUMMER
Anne Tedlock Brooks

A tale of mystery and romance and a girl who found both during one enchanted summer.

CLOUD OVER MALVERTON
Nancy Buckingham

Dulcie soon realises that something is seriously wrong at Malverton, and when violence strikes she is horrified to find herself under suspicion of murder.

AFTER THOUGHTS
Max Bygraves

The Cockney entertainer tells stories of his East End childhood, of his RAF days, and his post-war showbusiness successes and friendships with fellow comedians.

MOONLIGHT
AND MARCH ROSES
D. Y. Cameron

Lynn's search to trace a missing girl takes her to Spain, where she meets Clive Hendon. While untangling the situation, she untangles her emotions and decides on her own future.

NURSE ALICE IN LOVE
Theresa Charles

Accepting the post of nurse to little Fernie Sherrod, Alice Everton could not guess at the romance, suspense and danger which lay ahead at the Sherrod's isolated estate.

POIROT INVESTIGATES
Agatha Christie

Two things bind these eleven stories together — the brilliance and uncanny skill of the diminutive Belgian detective, and the stupidity of his Watson-like partner, Captain Hastings.

LET LOOSE THE TIGERS
Josephine Cox

Queenie promised to find the long-lost son of the frail, elderly murderess, Hannah Jason. But her enquiries threatened to unlock the cage where crucial secrets had long been held captive.